Forgotten Footprints

D1439476

3 8002 02351 618 2

Also by Rosemary Hayes
published by Troika Books

The Blue-Eyed Aborigine
The Mark

Forgotten Footprints

ROSEMARY HAYES

troika

For Richard Smart

Published by TROIKA

First published in the UK in 2017

Troika Books Ltd

Well House, Green Lane, Ardleigh CO7 7PD, UK

www.troikabooks.com

Text copyright © Rosemary Hayes 2016

The moral right of the author has been asserted

All rights reserved

A CIP catalogue record for this book is available

from the British Library

ISBN 978-1-909991-49-1

1 2 3 4 5 6 7 8 9 10

Printed in Poland

Pale feet that passed this way unnoticed.
Footprints of ghosts whose imprint was so light
That they merged with the land.

Coventry City Council CEN*	
3 8002 02351 618 2	
Askews & Holts	Oct-2017
	£6.99

Chapter One

August 1711

'Lord, how I hate this cabin!'

Annie Jansz was lying on a short plank with built up sides. There was only a thin straw mattress to protect her from the hard wood and she squirmed this way and that, trying to get comfortable.

'Ouch!' she said, as she banged her elbow.

She tried to sit up but she hit her head with such force that she fell back again.

'God in heaven, it's enough to try the patience of a saint.'

Her mother spoke from the other side of the cabin. 'Hush, Annie, and I'll thank you not to take the Lord's name in vain.'

Annie shifted so she could peer over the edge of her bunk.

'I thought you were asleep, Mother. Are you feeling better?'

Susan Jansz sighed. 'A little.'

Annie stayed where she was for a moment, staring gloomily around. Their servant, May, slept below her and her parents across from them. There was only a small space on the floor between the two sets of bunks – hardly sufficient to turn around, let alone to squat and relieve yourself.

Three weeks. They'd been at sea for three weeks, the four of them trapped on board at the mercy of the wind and sea, all crammed into this stifling cabin, rank with the stink of stale sweat, vomit and vapours from the piss pot. The stench of it turned her stomach.

And there were months more of this discomfort ahead of them.

How shall we endure it?

She withdrew her head and lay back, glad her father wasn't with them at this moment, filling the place with his bulk and wearing them out with his enthusiasm.

Why had they believed him? Why did they *always* believe him?

She thought back to the day he'd told them of his plan, his face flushed, his hat askew as he'd crashed into their little damp house in Zeeland.

'The VOC* have offered me a job,' he'd announced. 'A job in the East, overseeing their warehouses in Java.' He'd grabbed Annie round the waist and lifted her off her feet.

'Just imagine,' he'd said, putting her down at last and rubbing his hands together. 'We shall make a new life there and be rich; we shall see wonderful sights on the voyage; what an adventure it will be.'

Annie's mother had been horrified. 'God in heaven, Andries, you'll be the ruin of us all. Have you given no thought to the danger of such a voyage? And what of poor Annie? What life will there be for her in such an outlandish place?'

'She'll love it, Susan, and so will you. You'll be captivated by the wonders of the East. Such an opportunity for us all.'

'Will you really make your fortune, Father?' Annie had asked, looking up at his large ruddy face. He'd put his arm round her shoulders. 'Of course, girl. Of course I shall. We'll spend a few years in Java and then we'll return home to Zeeland rich and respected.'

He'd paced around the room, setting them afire with talk of exotic islands, of spices, brightly coloured

---

* VOC stood for 'Verenigde Oost-Indische Compagnie' or 'The United Dutch East India Company'.

birds, warm seas and the money he would make. And, of course, as usual, he had charmed them into believing that this time his scheme would work, this time he really would make his fortune.

Only their servant, May, refused to be beguiled.

'Lord, Mistress Annie,' she'd said. 'Half the folk who go out on those ships never return; there's shipwrecks and disease and fearsome heat – and tales of pirates and storms and all manner of horrors.'

But when Annie went down to the harbour with her father, she'd not been able to hide her excitement as she'd stared up at the great ship that was to take them on their voyage.

The *Zuytdorp* was the largest of the VOC's East Indiamen, a magnificent vessel with its beautiful curving line, spectacular decoration, colourful paintwork and flags and streamers. From the outside, it was certainly grand and beautiful.

There were other ships in the fleet, of all shapes and sizes, but the *Zuytdorp* was by far the grandest of them all.

'Lord, Father,' she'd stuttered.

He had squeezed her shoulder. 'Is she not magnificent, Annie? Imagine what adventures we'll have!'

And it *had* been exciting when they had finally sailed out of the harbour and watched the coastline grow smaller until it finally vanished.

But the excitement soon died.

It was bad enough for them, and they were privileged passengers – so Annie couldn't imagine what conditions were like for the sailors and soldiers on the lower decks.

She heaved herself off her plank and slid towards the floor, catching May's ample bottom with her foot on the way down.

May sat up in the bunk below hers and immediately banged her head.

'Ow! Mind where you put your foot, Mistress Annie! I don't need any more bruises on my poor body.' She rubbed her head with one hand and her bottom with the other.

'Oh, hold your peace, May, I didn't hurt you.'

May sniffed. 'I hate it here. I hate the sea, I hate the ship, I hate the cabin,' she muttered. 'And I still feel sick.'

She'd been saying the same thing every day since they left Zeeland. Annie took no notice. At first she'd been sympathetic. The seas had been rough and the ship had pitched and rolled horribly. Each one of them had suffered with seasickness, but May and Susan had been ill for longer, vomiting, retching and moaning for days on end. May was better now, but she still insisted she was too weak to work.

'For someone feeling sick, you're keeping down a good deal of victuals,' said Annie, sharply. She steadied herself on May's shoulder and then crouched down and opened the wooden chest that took up most of the space on the cabin floor and pulled out her cloak and cap. The clothes in the chest were damp but there was nowhere else to store them.

'I'm going up on deck,' she said, pulling the heavy cloak round her shoulders and tying the cap under her chin. 'And you can clean this cabin while I'm gone.'

Annie's mother stirred in her bunk. She, too, had been sick, and she looked pale and drawn.

'Don't be too hard on her, Annie,' said Susan Jansz. 'She's not been well.'

'Everyone's been unwell, Mother. We've all been seasick.'

'Some of us suffer more than others, Annie.' Susan Jansz's voice was weary. 'Now go and join your father on deck and take the air; it might improve your temper.'

Once she was free of the fetid atmosphere in the cabin, Annie felt better – and more inclined to be sorry for May, who had been brought so unwillingly on this voyage. She was a good companion, May, and though, at seventeen, only two years older than Annie, she was less innocent of the ways of the world and protective of the younger girl. Annie and May got along most of the time, except when May was in love – and then she was a worse dreamer than Father.

Annie squared her shoulders and climbed the ladder up on to the poop deck. Maybe this time, their fortunes really would change. Maybe this job in Java really would be a turning point.

Maybe. If they survived the journey.

She scrambled out on to the deck and looked round for her father but couldn't see him among all the sailors scurrying hither and thither.

The weather had been unseasonably cold for August and a damp, clinging fog had been with them for days. Life on board was pretty monotonous but at least up on deck things were always going on – and on the water, too, you could sometimes see passing ships. Father had identified them for her – Dutch, Danish and Scottish ships, fishing boats. All sorts of vessels had slid silently past them on the grey horizon.

She heard the sound of a gun being fired in the distance so that the ships of their fleet could locate each other and stay together. It sounded eerie coming out of the swirling fog and she shivered and wrapped her cloak more tightly round her body as she staggered over to the wooden railing, nearly colliding with the ship's boy, Lucas, as he scuttled past, his head lowered and his scrawny arms dragged down with heavy buckets from the officers' cabins. He was only about twelve; his hair was matted, he had sores on his hands and legs, his nose was running and his clothes were thin – far too thin for this damp, chilling weather. He looked hardly strong enough to carry the buckets. At his heels was the ship's cat, another scrawny specimen. Annie smiled at Lucas but he didn't look up.

She reached the railing and clung to it, breathing in the salty air. It was damp out here but at least the air was fresh. The decks were always seething with activity but today it seemed more frantic than usual, with constant shouting from the seamen aloft in the rigging and the men below hauling in sails to slow down the ship.

Further along the poop deck she saw the captain, and she shrunk against the railing, hoping he wouldn't notice her. She was scared of Captain Wysvliet – he'd already made it clear that the passengers on his ship were to keep out of the way as much as possible – but luckily he was too preoccupied to treat her to one of his fearsome scowls. His telescope was clamped to his eye and he was staring out across the water. Annie followed his gaze and saw the reason why the ship had almost come to a standstill.

She could just make out a boat being rowed across to the *Zuytdorp* and a few minutes later some seamen let down a rope ladder over the side. The captain lowered his telescope and strode past Annie down to the main deck to greet the visitor.

How do seamen do that? thought Annie. *How can they be so sure footed on deck when the roll of the ship always makes me stagger?*

Annie followed him, curious to see who was coming on board, and when she reached the main deck she flattened herself against the mast. She'd learnt quickly that if you didn't keep out of the way, you could easily be knocked into and then cursed.

Some of the other officers had gathered to greet the visitor, so he must be important.

Annie frowned. There was that cocky midshipman, François de Bruijn. He *would* be the only one who noticed her. He looked straight at her and grinned. Irritated, Annie found herself blushing. *Stupid, arrogant boy! He's only eighteen. Who does he think he is?*

She heard Captain Wysvliet's voice.

'Captain Blaauw, welcome on board.'

So that's who it was! Captain Blaauw, the captain of their sister ship, the *Belvliet* – the ship that would travel with them all the way to the Cape of Good Hope.

Captain Wysvliet dismissed the other officers and he and Blaauw made their way from the main deck to the quarterdeck, where they paced up and down, deep in conversation, their words mingling with the noises from the animals there. Annie hated to see the cows and pigs penned into such a small space, even though she enjoyed the meat they provided for the captain's table.

She slid down and sat on the deck, her back resting against the mainmast just underneath the quarterdeck. There was a bit of shelter here and at least she was out of everyone's way.

Was this what it was going to be like for the next few months? Monotonous, uncomfortable, living and sleeping in that cramped, miserable little cabin, with nothing to do?

She could hear the measured tread of the two captains and their murmured conversation, but at first it was only a background to her thoughts. And then, suddenly, the footsteps stopped and the men were right above her, leaning on the balustrade which divided the two decks. She kept very still. Surely they could see her crouching only a few feet below them? She didn't know what to do. Should she stand up and walk away, with as much dignity as she could muster? No, she would feel too foolish. She decided to stay where she was and made herself as small and as quiet as she could. She could hear their words clearly.

Wysvliet was speaking. 'This news. Are you sure it is reliable, man?'

'Certain,' replied Captain Blaauw. 'I have it on the best authority. The returning fleet have already reached Holland.'

'And the supply ships never made contact?'

Blaauw laughed. 'No, they are still at sea – and still full.'

'Then, it is our good luck,' said Wysvliet, quietly. 'If we play our cards right, my friend, we shall make a good many extra guilders from this.'

'Especially if we keep the crews on short rations,' replied Blaauw.

Then there were some remarks between the men about rotten ship's biscuit and bread that seemed to amuse them greatly. They both burst into laughter.

'Come,' said Captain Wysvliet at last. 'We'll go to my cabin and drink to our good fortune.'

When Annie was sure they were gone, she stood up slowly and lurched across the main deck to the rail. She was frowning. She had made no sense of this conversation but its tone had left her feeling uneasy. She didn't like Captain Wysvliet. What was he plotting with his fellow captain?

'Hear any secrets, Annie?'

She whipped round and found herself looking into the grinning face of the midshipman, François de Bruijn. Curse the boy! Why was he always creeping up on her?

'Of course not,' she said crossly. 'And anyway, I wouldn't eavesdrop.'

François raised an eyebrow. 'Umm,' he said.

'What do you mean, "umm"?'

'I was watching you, Annie. You were listening very carefully. Are you sure you didn't overhear something?'

'No I didn't. And anyway, why should talk between the captains interest me? It's none of my business.'

François laughed. 'I'm only teasing you, Annie. Don't take my remarks to heart.' Then he turned and began to walk off. 'Why don't you go and find your father?' he said, over his shoulder. 'He's up on the forecastle deck talking to the surgeon.'

Annie stayed where she was. She wasn't going to take orders from François de Bruijn. She had to admit that he was a handsome boy, but she hated his assurance and arrogance. She'd heard rumours that he was from a wealthy Norwegian family, so no doubt he was destined for a glorious career at sea – and didn't he know it! He was obviously educated; his Dutch was fluent. She frowned. He might be clever and rich but he certainly needed taking down a peg or two.

She watched as one of the cabin boys emerged from the galley with a tray laden with wine and cheese, made his way carefully up to the poop deck and then disappeared into the captain's cabin. Although she'd told François that she wasn't interested in what the two captains were saying to one another, that wasn't true. Her curiosity had been whetted.

Her thoughts were interrupted by May, who

advanced crab-like over the deck towards her and then grabbed her round the waist. Annie frowned at her. 'I thought you were cleaning the cabin,' she said.

'Oh, let a girl get her breath back at least, Mistress Annie. I'm not used to walking on something that lurches beneath me; give me dry land every time.'

She adjusted her cap. 'And before you start, I *am* going to clean the cabin – but there's nothing down there for such work so I'm off to beg a bit of vinegar and some rags.'

Such practicalities hadn't occurred to Annie. 'Where from?' she asked.

May smiled. 'Well,' she said slowly, 'I've spotted this good looking sailor who works in the galley . . .'

'*May!*'

Later that day, Annie and her parents dined at the captain's table. It was the first time that Susan Jansz had felt well enough to emerge from their cabin, and she still looked pale and walked unsteadily.

'Are you all right, Mother?' asked Annie, as she held her arm.

'A lot better for being out of that cursed bunk at last.'

There were quite a crowd of them at table: Annie and her parents; Captain Wysvliet; Melchior Haijensz, the uppersteersman; Jan Liebent, a VOC undermerchant; the master surgeon; the preacher, and some other passengers.

Captain Wysvliet was in high spirits, laughing with his neighbours, ordering more wine, complimenting the women.

The surgeon, Jacob Hendricx, was sitting next to Annie. Annie liked the man. He always made a point of talking to her and not ignoring her as some of the other officers did.

'The captain seems in a merry mood,' he whispered to her.

Wysvliet was often dour and uncommunicative at dinner, so his behaviour was all the more unusual. Annie was more certain than ever that he and Blaauw were hatching some plot for their mutual gain. But she wasn't going to say anything about it – at least, not yet – so she changed the subject.

'Are you being kept busy, sir?'

Jacob smiled. 'At the moment I have one case of pneumonia, but the rest are all chest ailments,' he said.

'Is that because it is so unseasonably cold?' she asked.

'Yes, indeed.' He hesitated, then continued, lowering his voice, 'And because some of the recruits are not supplied with suitable clothing, so they have nothing to protect them from the weather.'

She was horrified. 'But how can that happen?'

Jacob sighed and fiddled with the piece of cheese on his platter. 'Well, often these boys are recruited by innkeepers at home, who make money out of it. They only give them thin clothes, assuring the recruit that these will be sufficient for the tropics.' He gave a mirthless laugh. 'The scoundrels don't mention the time they will spend in this cold North Sea.' Then he added, 'If only we were not still at war with the French and Spanish, then we could have taken the shorter route, and not lost so much precious time.'

'The shorter route?'

'Aye, Annie, the shorter route through the channel between France and England. In these uncertain times it is too risky, the waters too narrow, and the *Zuytdorp* would be a rich prize for enemy ships.'

Annie had little knowledge of where countries lay but she nodded and thought again of young Lucas, the ship's boy, shivering in his thin shirt, his nose running and his skin covered with sores.

'Do the recruits not question these innkeepers?'

Jacob shook his head. 'No, they are ignorant lads, Annie, and they know no better. Most of them have no idea of what lies beyond their own town, let alone their own country.'

Annie took a mouthful of beef and chewed it thoughtfully, painfully aware of how little she knew, either. Then she picked up the glass in front of her and swilled down the beef with some wine.

'But it will be better for them soon, won't it? Once we are heading south the weather will improve. And they'll be plenty warm enough when we reach the tropics.'

Jacob looked at her kindly. 'Ah, Annie, they will be warm enough then, to be sure, but I tell you, when we reach the tropics, my job will be a good deal harder.'

Chapter Two

Early the next morning, Annie's father came crashing into the cabin.

'Hurry, Annie, come up on deck. It's a beautiful morning at last. The fog's gone and there's so much happening up on deck.' He turned to his wife. 'And you, Susan. The air will do you good.'

Annie looked up from her needlework. It was the first time that the light from the small window had been bright enough for her to see the fine stitching. She put it down and stretched.

'Why, what's happening?'

'We're taking on more supplies,' he said. 'It appears that our beer and water is running low and that there is some infestation in the bread and some other problems with the food.'

Annie thought back to the conversation between the two captains and remembered how they had laughed when infested bread had been mentioned.

Susan Jansz frowned. 'But I understood that we had supplies on board to last us until we reached the Cape?'

Andries shrugged. 'I'm sure the captain knows what he is doing, Susan. He is thinking of our wellbeing and taking on board these extra victuals that have so conveniently come our way.'

'But I don't understand,' said Susan. 'Where have they come from?'

'It appears that the cruiser and the hooker going out to revictual the fleet missed their rendezvous. The fleet are already back in Holland.'

'So these extra supplies aren't needed?' said Annie.

'Not by the returning fleet, no. But we shall make good use of them.'

Annie said nothing. Thoughtfully, she put away her needlework and made ready to go up on deck.

'Are you coming, Mother?'

Susan Jansz sighed. 'Not now, dear. I'll rest a bit.'

'You're not still feeling sick, are you?'

'A little, dear. But I'm sure it will pass. Perhaps you can find May and tell her to fetch me a wine caudle.'

Annie followed her father out on to the main deck. Her spirits rose as she saw the blue sky. The wind had changed, the fog had dispersed and, although there was still a chill in the air, it felt dry and fresh. She took a deep breath of the refreshing air, then she and her father found an out of the way spot where they could watch all the activity.

Suddenly, Andries grabbed Annie's arm. 'Look, Annie.' He was pointing to a spot a little beyond the supply ships.

Annie gasped as she saw five or six large sea creatures, leaping and playing around the boats. 'What are they, Father? Are they dangerous?'

Andries laughed. 'Why no, Annie – they are dolphins. They are curious creatures, come to see what's happening.'

Annie watched them for some time, leaping gracefully out of the water and diving back in again, and then as suddenly as they had appeared, they vanished, and she turned her attention to the human activity around her.

Dwarfed by the huge bulk of the *Zuytdorp*, the two supply ships were lying alongside. Officers were directing the men to heave the barrels of water and beer, dried peas and bread up from the supply ships and on to the deck, then roll them towards the hatchway where more sailors were taking them down to the hold, grunting and swearing with the effort of moving such heavy cargo.

'There's so much!' said Annie. 'Surely we don't need all this?'

'No doubt some of it will be for the *Belvliet*,' said her father.

'Are *their* supplies running low, too? And is *their* bread infested, too?'

'It would seem so, Annie.'

'How surprising that both ships should have the same shortages,' she said.

Her father didn't notice the sarcasm in her voice. He had just seen the preacher and was walking away towards him. Annie noticed May emerging from the galley, and she beckoned her over.

'What have you been doing in there, May?' she asked. May adjusted her cap and grinned. 'As if I didn't know,' whispered Annie, poking May sharply. 'Mother needs you,' she said, more loudly. 'She wants you to fetch her a wine caudle.'

'Oh, I shall have to go back to the galley to fetch it, then,' said May, winking.

Annie raised her eyes to the sky. 'What's his name, May?'

May giggled. 'He's called Jan – and he's one of the cooks.'

'One of the cooks, eh? And what does he say about all these extra victuals being brought on board?'

May came closer and said, in a confidential whisper,

'He can't understand it. He says there's plenty here already and as far as he knows, it's in good condition. He doesn't see the need for any more.'

Annie didn't reply.

'I'd better fetch that wine caudle for your poor mother then, Mistress Annie.'

Annie nodded. 'Thank you, May. And don't dawdle in the galley after it's been mixed!'

Father was deep in conversation with the preacher and for the moment the business of offloading the barrels had come to a halt while the men rested, propped up against coils of rope, smoking clay pipes.

Annie seized her chance. After checking that no one was looking in her direction, she slipped away and ducked down the hatchway that led to the lower decks. She scuttled past the gun deck, peering nervously into the gloom to see the crowded conditions, with hammocks slung side by side. Some of the sailors were sitting and talking in groups, some lay in their hammocks and some were upright, albeit stooped over, unable to stand up straight as they shuffled about, either side of the huge cannons. The stench made her gag. She knew that the crew were supposed to relieve themselves overboard, but it was clear that this didn't always happen.

She climbed down further, to the orlop deck, where there was even less headroom. This was where the surgeon had his cabin and dispensary and where the midshipmen and junior officers were quartered, too. With her heart in her mouth, expecting to be challenged at any moment, she kept going, moving as quietly and quickly as she could, still further down.

No one saw her as she reached the hold, in the bowels of the ship, where all the cargo was stored. She knew that the hold was usually well guarded but now, with seamen going to and fro and extra cargo being stored there, this might be her one chance to see what the ship was carrying.

She was right. Although there were plenty of people about, they were mostly busy rearranging all the extra barrels that had been brought on board and no one noticed her as she crept into a dark corner to hide. It was very gloomy and she couldn't see the faces of the men shifting the goods so she hoped that they wouldn't be able to see her either.

She crouched quietly in her hiding place for a while, listening to the cursing and groaning and general banter.

Then she heard the clatter of another person coming down to the hold, apparently unencumbered by any cargo, for the footsteps were quick and light. The men continued to talk and shunt the cargo about, but suddenly an imperious voice cut through the noise.

'Silence! I am charged to make a record of everything

here – new and old. You there – and you! Check the quantities while I read out the manifest.'

Annie froze. It was that cocky midshipman, François de Bruijn! *Please don't let him see me*, she thought, shrinking even further into the shadows and flattening herself against the hull.

There was some mumbling and more shifting of heavy containers, then someone lit a lantern and Annie could see more clearly. François was holding a list of some sort up to the lantern. He cleared his throat and started calling out the items.

His voice droned on, stopping after every item to make sure it was there and that the quantities were accurate, and waiting for an 'Aye,' from the men checking the goods. The list was endless: wine, beer, butter, meat, bacon, dried peas and beans, cheese, herring, ship's biscuit, groats and various oils. Then sheets and ingots of lead, cloth, rope, sulphur, pitch, canvas, paper, muskets, leather, copper, salt, candles, iron hoops and plates. In the cavernous hold, he and the men checked the goods, moving hither and thither, sometimes so far from Annie that she could only faintly hear their voices.

While all this was being re-counted and listed, other men were shifting some heavy chests quite close to Annie, to make room for the extra supplies. She shuffled forward a bit to get a closer look, wondering what might be in them and, as she moved forward, a splinter of wood caught the flesh of her hand. She cried out with the pain of it and then immediately put her hand over her mouth.

There was a sudden silence, then the sound of purposeful footsteps coming towards her. François grabbed her by the arm.

'What do you think you're doing, Annie? You know passengers aren't allowed down here.'

'Let go of me,' she hissed, pulling her arm out of his grip. 'I only wanted to see what we are carrying.'

'Well, now you've seen. Off you go; back to your cabin.'

Angrily, Annie pulled her arm free, blushing with humiliation. She pointed at the heavy chests. 'What's inside them?'

'Money,' said François, shortly. 'Chests and chests full of newly minted silver. Two hundred and fifty thousand guilders.'

Annie gasped. 'Two hundred and fifty thousand guilders! What's all that money for?'

'You ignorant girl – what do you think it's for? For paying for the spices we shall bring back and all the other goods from the East. And for paying the folk at the garrison in Java.'

Annie bit her lip. She was about to protest that she was far from ignorant, but she swallowed her angry retort, afraid that François might report her if she angered him.

'And every last ducat is counted,' continued François. 'So don't think of stealing any.'

Annie couldn't contain herself. She scowled into the darkness. 'What a thing to say! As if I would.'

François laughed. 'You're very easy to tease, Annie,' he said. Then his voice became stern again. 'Now,' he continued. 'I'll pretend I've not seen you but you'd better get back to your cabin before any of the other officers come down here, or you'll be in real trouble.'

'Maddening boy,' Annie muttered to herself. 'Other officers, indeed!' She knew François wasn't an officer – not yet, anyway. The surgeon had told her that he wasn't old enough to take his lieutenant's exams, because he was only eighteen. Not that it was of any interest to her!

Annie came out from her hiding place and stood upright. Some of the sailors working in the hold turned to stare at her and she could hear their murmurings and sniggers, and it dawned on her why the passengers – particularly the women – were not encouraged to stray from the upper decks. She had to admit that, at that moment, she was glad of François's presence.

He turned to the men. 'Back to work,' he said harshly, and started checking off the supplies again.

Going back to the upper decks wasn't as easy as

coming down. The rest period on the main deck had finished and the seamen were bringing the goods down through the hatchways again. Annie had to flatten herself to let the sailors pass and some of them deliberately pressed themselves against her, grinning and saying, 'Beg pardon, miss,' as they did so. By the time she reached the gun deck, she was flustered, blushing and perspiring. Everywhere she looked there seemed to be men leering at her. She was near to tears when May found her cowering at the bottom of the ladder, making way for yet another burly seaman.

'For heaven's sakes, Mistress Annie,' shouted May, peering down the hatchway at her. 'What are you doing down there? I've been looking for you everywhere.' She grabbed Annie's hand and hauled her up.

'Let my mistress pass, you great lout,' she shouted at the man who was trying to go down. The man grinned at May and made a lewd remark, but she ignored him. 'Come on, Mistress Annie, this is no place for you.'

'Thank you, May,' gasped Annie as they emerged at last on to the main deck. May rolled her eyes at her. 'Whatever possessed you to go exploring down there?' she said. 'You have no idea how rough these men can be.'

'I have now,' said Annie, straightening her cap and smoothing down her skirt.

'What am I to tell your parents?' asked May. 'I was

sent to find you and they'll wonder why I've been so long.'

'You'll tell them nothing, May,' said Annie sharply, recovering her dignity.

May looked at her. 'Oh, come now, Mistress Annie, I must tell them something – or they'll blame me for dawdling.'

'Oh, all right. Make up some excuse. Tell them I was speaking with the master surgeon and you didn't want to disturb me.'

There was an uneasy silence while May regarded Annie, a sly smile on her face. 'If you want me to lie for you, Mistress Annie,' she said, 'then you'll have to tell me what you were doing down there.'

'I wanted to see what is stored in the hold,' said Annie, crossly. 'And now I have. That's all there is to it.'

'So what's it worth, not to tell your parents where you were?'

Annie turned on her. 'Don't you try and bargain with me, May. If you dare mention this to my parents, I shall tell them of all the time you spend flirting with your Jan in the galley when you should be seeing to our needs.'

They glared at each other but then, finally, Annie relented and put her hand on May's arm. 'I admit I was never more glad to see you, May,' she said. 'Thank you for coming to my rescue just now.'

'You're too innocent to be among those rough seamen, Mistress Annie. And I tell you, the soldiers are worse. The likes of me – well, I know how to deal with them, I can look after myself. But you – you should stick to that nice young midshipman.'

'What young midshipman? What are you talking about?'

May nudged her. 'I've seen you chatting to that young François de Bruijn. And I've seen the way he looks at you, too.'

Annie felt the blood rise to her cheeks. 'Don't be ridiculous!' she said.

'There,' said May. 'You're blushing.'

'I am not!'

May grinned. 'Well, we'd better go and find your parents, Mistress Annie, and tell them all about this long conversation you've been having with the master surgeon.'

Later that day, Annie went looking for the Master Surgeon, but he wasn't on the main decks and she guessed he would be at his dispensary on the orlop deck. She certainly wasn't going down there again, so she would have to wait in order to speak to him, to give credence to the story she and May had told her parents.

She was about to return to the cabin when she

spotted Lucas, the ship's boy. He had been feeding the animals that were wretchedly corralled on the quarterdeck and now he was squatting in the corner of their pen, watching them eat.

Annie climbed up to the quarterdeck and went over to the pen. The stench was worse than the gun deck and Annie's eyes started to smart. A cow mooed loudly as she approached and Lucas looked up. He started to struggle to his feet.

'Don't get up, Lucas. Are you off duty now?'

He looked terrified. 'Sorry, mistress, I shouldn't be here,' he mumbled. 'I've finished my work. I'd best go below.'

He grabbed the empty feed bucket and clambered out of the pen. Annie noticed that his sores were no better and that his nose was still running. And, close to, his small body was rake thin, the bones showing through at his wrists and ankles.

'Don't go, Lucas. I want to ask you something.'

Lucas stood with his back to the pen, his eyes downcast. 'Don't be frightened,' said Annie gently. 'You've done nothing wrong.' She sat down and patted the deck beside her. 'Sit down for a moment.'

Nervously, he lowered himself to the deck, clutching the empty bucket. Annie saw that he was still dressed in his thin shirt. 'Have you any warmer clothes, Lucas? Your shirt and breeks are very thin.'

Lucas kept his eyes on the ground. 'These are all I have, miss,' he muttered.

'And have you seen the ship's surgeon about those sores on your arms and legs?'

Lucas tucked his legs up under his knees, hiding his sores from view as well as he could. He shook his head.

'You should, Lucas. The surgeon can give you something to heal them.'

Lucas shook his head again. 'I don't want to go bothering an officer,' he said, and his voice was so low that Annie had difficulty hearing him.

'But the surgeon is here to look after the crew, Lucas. That's his job. He sees the sick every morning after prayers, down there, by the mainmast.'

Lucas said nothing.

Annie spoke again. 'Do you look after these animals by yourself?'

He nodded.

'You're doing a very good job. They are healthy beasts.'

The ghost of a smile flickered over his lips.

'And what of your other duties?'

Lucas wiped his nose with the back of his hand and then rubbed the snot off on his breeks.

'I help swab the gun deck and such. And other cleaning. Whatever I'm told to do.'

All the dirtiest jobs, thought Annie.

She looked at him. 'Can you read, Lucas?'

His head jerked up and, for the first time, he met her eyes. There was genuine astonishment on his face.

'Read? Me? No, miss, reading's not for the likes of me.'

Annie got slowly to her feet. 'I'm going to see if I can find some warmer clothes for you, Lucas.'

Suddenly, Lucas became animated. 'No, no – please, miss, please don't. It won't do no good. They'll just take them from me.'

She frowned. 'Who will take them from you?'

He hung his head. 'I can't say.'

Annie sighed. 'Will you go and see the surgeon after morning prayers tomorrow, at least?' she said.

Lucas ducked his head and then scuttled away.

Chapter Three

It was late that afternoon when Annie finally managed to speak to the surgeon. She saw him coming up on deck from below and she went over to him. She almost fell in her eagerness to reach him and he put out an arm to steady her.

'Not so fast, Annie,' he said, laughing. 'You must learn to walk slowly around these treacherous decks, or you'll measure your length.'

'I've been looking for you all day,' she said breathlessly. 'I need to speak to you.'

Jacob frowned. 'What is so urgent, Annie? Is your mother still sick?'

'No. No, it's not that. Well, she is feeling a bit sick still, but it only troubles her in the mornings.'

'Ah. In the mornings only? Is there . . .' Then he

stopped. 'I'm sorry, Annie, I'm forgetting myself. So, if it's not your mother, what is troubling you?'

'I have a confession.'

Jacob looked alarmed. 'A confession?'

'Yes. You see, I lied to my parents. I told them I was speaking with you when I wasn't!'

Jacob smiled. 'And why was that, if I may ask?'

Annie blushed and looked down at her feet. 'I went exploring. I wanted to see what was being stored in the hold. May was sent to look for me and couldn't find me, so we made up this story about me having a long talk to you and her not wanting to disturb our conversation.'

'Oh dear, Annie, such deceit! You are far too curious, and I can see why you don't want to tell your parents the truth; the lower decks are no place for a young girl.'

'I know that now,' said Annie ruefully. 'But will you support my story? If my father should ask you, will you say that we have had a long conversation?'

'I won't lie for you, Annie,' said Jacob. 'But I'm happy to have that long conversation now, if it helps. I've come up on deck to take the air for a while and I could do with some lively discourse.'

They walked over to the rail together. Jacob stretched and took a deep breath. 'So, what did you discover about our cargo, Annie?'

'I had no idea that we carried so much. All those

newly minted coins, for a start.'

'Ah yes,' said Jacob. 'The Company has never sent so much money on one voyage, I believe.'

'And all the extra food and such from the supply ships. Do we really need all that, Jacob?'

He didn't answer at once. Then he said, slowly, 'Yes, that is curious.'

Annie watched his face carefully but it gave nothing away. They stood together in companionable silence, looking out across the water. The sun was glinting on the waves and gulls were shrieking overhead as they fought over some scrap of food. Annie loosened her cloak.

'It is beginning to feel warmer at last,' she said.

'Aye. Soon we shall be heading south along the coast of Portugal, and you'll feel a lot warmer then.'

'And so will poor Lucas,' she said.

'Lucas?'

'He's the ship's boy, one of those recruits you told me of. You know – duped by the innkeepers. He told me he has but the one set of clothes.'

Jacob nodded. 'Poor boy. He's one of many.'

'But that's not all. His nose is running and he is covered with sores.'

'Then he should come to see me after morning prayers. He must know that that is when I see the walking sick.'

Annie nodded. 'I told him, but he's a nervous lad. He said he didn't want to bother an officer.'

Jacob clicked his tongue in exasperation. 'Stupid child. Then I shall send for him myself.'

'Thank you,' said Annie. 'He's such a timid lad – and he has all the dirtiest jobs. And he's never learnt his letters, either.'

Jacob shrugged. 'Very few of the crew have,' he said. 'But what of you, Annie? Are you a reader? Is that how you pass your time – when you're not creeping down to the hold to check on the cargo?'

She laughed. 'I won't do that again, I promise. And yes, I read to while away the time, and do some needlework. But Father owns very few books and most are too boring for me – they're all about business and making money.'

'Then you should borrow a title or two from young François de Bruijn. He has quite a library on board.'

'Huh!' said Annie. 'No doubt all in Norwegian.'

'Not so,' said Jacob. 'He's very well educated, you know, Annie. He reads in several languages. Why, he even has pamphlets written by that famous Englishman, Defoe.'

Annie said nothing. She was certainly not going to ask François if she could borrow anything from him. She abruptly changed the subject.

'How is your patient with pneumonia?' she asked.

Jacob sighed. 'Worse, I'm afraid. There is nothing more I can do for him. His fate is in God's hands now.'

'I am sorry to hear that. And are there others who are very sick?'

'A few, but none as bad as him.'

'So, you are still mainly treating colds and sores?'

'Aye, plenty of them. And injuries sustained on board. Sailors and soldiers who miss their footing and fall, injuries from fighting between men, injuries from the whip.'

Annie flinched. She knew that the men were punished from time to time. Already she'd seen men whipped publicly, though she always turned away from the sight.

'Doesn't it seem contrary to cause men injury through the whip?' she asked.

'I don't care to witness punishments being meted out, Annie. I am a healer. But discipline on board ship is essential. Just imagine what would happen if discipline was not maintained.'

Annie shivered, even though she was warmer now. 'What do they do, these soldiers and seamen, that merit the whip?'

Jacob shrugged. 'Falling asleep on duty is one of the worst crimes – and refusing to obey orders, of course. And for unclean behaviour. These are some of the commonest.'

Annie thought back to the stink from the gun deck. Did 'unclean behaviour' mean relieving yourself in the place where you ate and slept? Probably. She didn't like to dwell on these things – either the punishments or the crimes.

'Do you have anyone to help you in your work, Jacob?'

He nodded. 'Yes, I have been assigned an assistant from the crew. He's called Baernt Dannekeand.' He paused. 'He's a clumsy lad, but he's strong and, God willing, his skills will improve. I shall need all the help I can get when we reach the tropics.'

'I could help you,' said Annie, eagerly. 'I'm not clumsy, and I nursed Mother and May when they were so ill at the beginning of the voyage. I don't mind the sight of gore and vomit. Oh, please say I can help you, Jacob. I'm so bored!'

Jacob laughed out loud. 'Oh, Annie, what an idea! A young girl, down on the orlop deck. Have you already forgotten your experience this morning?'

Annie bit her lip. 'But . . . but if I was with you, no one would dare treat me . . . badly. And I could be a real help.'

Jacob put his hand on her shoulder. 'I am touched, Annie, that you should want to help in my work, but believe me, a surgeon's assistant is no job for a girl. And anyway, your father would never allow it.'

Annie didn't reply. The germ of an idea had lodged in her mind.

'But if you want something to occupy yourself, Annie,' went on Jacob, 'why don't you try to teach that young Lucas of yours his letters?'

She clapped her hands. 'That's a capital idea! I'd like to do that.' She smiled, remembering Lucas's haste to escape her presence earlier. 'Though I'm not sure whether he would accept my help.'

Jacob took some deep breaths. 'Worth a try, surely? And it would keep you busy. Now, Annie,' he continued, 'you are an excellent companion and I have greatly enjoyed your company, but I must go back to my dispensary.'

The next morning, after prayers, Annie lingered on the main deck while Jacob and his assistant, Baernt, tended the walking sick. She watched Jacob carefully as he cleaned up sores, changed dressings and administered potions and ointment. He was gentle and thorough in his work, but Baernt was slow, rough and clumsy. Time and again, Jacob would have to redress a wound when Baernt had tied a bandage too tightly and, although Jacob never raised his voice, every time this happened, Baernt looked surly and rebellious.

I could do it so much better than him.

There was no sign of Lucas among those waiting

to be treated, and Annie tapped her foot impatiently. Stupid boy! Didn't he want to be cured of his wretched cold and sores? As the last of the men were dismissed back to their duties or to rest below, she approached Jacob.

'So Lucas has not presented himself for treatment?'

Jacob looked up. 'Ah, your little ship's boy. No, Annie, he has not. Thank you for reminding me about him.' He turned to his assistant.

'Baernt, will you go and fetch the ship's boy, Lucas, and bring him to me? You know him?'

Baernt frowned. He said 'Aye,' in a way that implied that Lucas was beneath contempt and left them, muttering under his breath.

Jacob sighed. 'Not the most willing of helpers, I'm afraid.'

'And, as you say, unskilled at his job,' said Annie. 'I watched you retying his bandages. You would have progressed quicker without him.'

'He may be clumsy, Annie,' said Jacob gently, 'but his strength will be very useful if we need to hold down a poor wretch to operate.'

Annie swallowed. 'Well, yes, that is a job I could never do. But I could certainly swab and bandage more handily than him.'

Jacob gave her a sideways look. 'The answer is still no, Annie.'

A little later, Baernt brought Lucas up from below. He was dragging him across the deck, and Lucas looked terrified.

'Let the poor boy go, Baernt,' said Jacob. 'You'll frighten him with your rough ways.'

Baernt said nothing but he let go of Lucas's arm and went over to the railing, cleared his throat and spat a great globule of phlegm overboard.

Jacob put his arm round Lucas's shoulders. 'Let me have a look at these sores, boy,' he said gently. Then he began to swab them with a clean rag dipped in alcohol. Lucas flinched when Jacob touched him, but he didn't cry out.

'Some of these are infected,' said Jacob. 'I'll clean them and bandage them, but you must come back every morning for the dressings to be changed, otherwise they won't heal.'

'And what of his running nose?' asked Annie, standing over him with her arms folded.

Jacob laughed. 'Don't tell me my job, Annie. I'm coming to that.' He turned back to his patient. 'Fortunately, Lucas, your chest is not affected, and your running nose will clear of its own accord now that the weather is improved.'

He called Baernt over. 'Start packing up now, Baernt.'

Slowly, Baernt started to replace bandages,

ointments and potions back into the surgeon's box. Annie watched him and her fingers itched to do the job. He crammed everything in without a thought, when she could see that it wouldn't all fit in if it wasn't properly packed. Unable to contain her irritation with the man, she bent down beside him.

'Here, let me,' she said. And before anyone could stop her, she had emptied the box and was rewinding bandages and slotting everything into its allocated space.

Baernt glared at her and Jacob turned away to hide his smile. When he turned back, he addressed Lucas.

'Now, Lucas, Mistress Annie has another plan for you.'

Lucas looked up nervously.

'Don't worry, boy, it is nothing unpleasant. She is going to teach you your letters.'

Lucas found his voice at last. 'Why? Why would you want to do that, mistress?'

Annie stared at him. It had never occurred to her that he wouldn't *want* to learn his letters.

'Because if you learn to read, Lucas, your life will be so much better.'

Baernt sneered at her. 'How's that, mistress? You think he'll become a clerk or some such? He's a ship's boy. He's the lowest of the low. He has no use for reading and never will have.'

'That's enough, Baernt,' said Jacob sharply. 'Now take my box back to the dispensary. I'll be there shortly.'

When Baernt had gone, Jacob turned to Lucas. 'Don't believe him, Lucas. Mistress Annie is right. Learning your letters will most certainly help you to better yourself.'

Lucas was looking down at his bare feet. He said nothing.

Annie knelt down and took his hands in hers. 'I would like to teach you, Lucas. Do you not want to learn?'

'Please, miss, I don't want no special treatment.'

What a strange thing to say, thought Annie.

But Jacob understood. 'Mistress Annie will be discreet, Lucas. No one else need know.'

Still Lucas said nothing.

'And I will make sure that Baernt keeps his mouth shut,' he added.

When Jacob and Lucas had gone back to their duties, Annie stayed on deck for a while. She couldn't understand why Lucas was so reluctant to be taught his letters. Well, whether he liked it or not, she was going to try and drum them into his head. She went off to beg writing materials from her father.

At dinner that evening, Annie was quiet. As usual,

the table was groaning with good food, but she had little appetite for it. She kept thinking of Lucas's thin wrists and ankles. Jacob was not present and she was seated next to the preacher, who made little effort to engage her in conversation. Her father was on her other side but he was busy chatting to one of the other women passengers, weaving a fine fantasy about how wonderful their lives would be once they arrived in Java. When he drew breath, she tugged at his sleeve. 'Where's the master surgeon?' she asked. 'Why is he not dining with us?'

The woman passenger had heard her question. 'Oh, apparently he is with a young German soldier who has pneumonia. The boy's not expected to live.' Her voice was bored and matter of fact.

She knows nothing of Jacob's work, thought Annie, *and cares less. But it will be another matter if she gets sick and needs his help.*

When the cheese was passed round, Annie took a large helping and then, as no one was paying her any attention, she slipped it into the pocket of her skirt, together with a hunk of bread. Perhaps bribing Lucas with food would make him keener to learn his letters.

A few days later, the young German soldier lost his fight with pneumonia, and Annie witnessed the first burial at sea.

All the seamen who were not on watch were assembled on the main deck, together with the passengers and soldiers. But the topmen, working in the highest yards, went on working aloft, and their shouts could be heard faintly, far above what was happening on deck, mingling with the preacher's words from the Bible as the boy's body, wrapped in canvas, was slipped overboard.

Annie went over to Jacob after the burial. He was looking sad.

'Such a waste of a young life.'

She couldn't think of anything to say, so she put her hand on his arm and he covered it with his own. 'I fear there'll be many more sea burials before we reach Java, Annie.'

As the *Zuytdorp* sailed down the coast of Portugal, the weather became much warmer and Annie spent more time up on deck. She had told her family about her decision to teach Lucas his letters and her father had approved. 'Good, Annie. It will give you some occupation; and the ignorant lad will be grateful for it.'

Susan, however, was not so enthusiastic. 'Do be careful, Annie. He could well be diseased. He could pass on some horrible sickness to us all.'

But Annie persisted. At first, Lucas had been so nervous that he'd been unable to take anything in, but gradually, sweetened by tasty scraps from the captain's table, he had begun to relax and was making a little progress. Every day, Annie would meet him on the quarterdeck, by the animals' pen, as soon as he had finished his feeding duties. The ship's cat soon learnt that Annie usually brought food with her so it, too, was present at the lessons, purring and rubbing itself on Lucas's legs.

'You love that cat, Lucas, don't you?' said Annie.

Lucas bent down to stroke it. 'It's like me. It gets nothing but kicks and punches from the crew, so we stick together.'

'Is life that bad for you, Lucas? Do they bully you?'

He shrugged. 'I'm the ship's boy. I'm nothing. I must expect blows from the others.'

'And what of food, Lucas? You don't get enough to eat, do you? I can tell from the way you wolf down the bread and cheese I bring you.'

'No one has enough food,' he muttered. 'They all complain, but what can they do?'

The words of the *Belvliet* captain came back to her. *'Especially if we keep the crew on short rations.'*

'It's not right, Lucas. We have ample food on board. I've seen it with my own eyes.'

'Oh, aye. The officers and the passengers are well fed, no doubt.'

He had misunderstood her, and she didn't tell him

about her trip down to the hold.

When they had finished their lesson for the day, Annie was thoughtful. Who should she tell about the captains' conversation? Who would have influence to change the situation? It was wrong that she and her family, the other passengers and the officers, even the midshipmen, had plenty of food, served on pewter platters, and wine in glass goblets, while the rest of the crew were on short rations.

She decided to tell Jacob of the conversation she had overheard but, as usual, he was nowhere to be found. As the day wore on, she became more and more angry and more and more determined to try and do something about it, so, when she saw François next, instead of avoiding him, as she usually did, she marched up to him.

'Do you know what the captain is doing?' she demanded.

François raised an eyebrow. 'What do you mean, Annie?'

She spelt it out. 'Captain Wysvliet is starving the crew so he can sell off spare victuals and line his own pocket when we reach Java.'

'Oh, yes,' said François coolly. 'And what proof do you have?'

'I heard them. That time when Captain Blaauw came on board. They were hatching the plan then.'

'I knew you were eavesdropping, Annie,' he said lazily. 'And anyway, he's not *starving* the crew. He's just keeping them short.'

Annie glared at him. 'You *know* this, and yet you do nothing about it?'

'There's nothing I *can* do, Annie. The captain is in charge of life on board ship. He gives the orders.'

'Huh! Your stomach is well fed, François. You wouldn't be so complacent if you were a hardworking crew member with no victuals to keep up your energy.'

François shrugged. 'It's not uncommon,' he said, matter of factly. 'I've seen it done before.'

'What do you mean, you've seen it done before? You can't have. This is your first voyage!'

François looked momentarily disconcerted.

'And anyway,' said Annie, stamping her foot. 'Even if it is not uncommon, it doesn't make it *right.*'

François folded his arms and looked down at her, grinning at her in the supercilious manner she hated so much. 'I've seen you smuggling food to your little ship's boy,' he said. 'You're doing him no favours, Annie, feeding him up and trying to teach him his letters. It will make the other boys jealous and they'll pick on him even more. He's just a pet for you, isn't he? Like that scrawny cat I've seen you feeding.'

'How *dare* you speak of Lucas in that way!' shouted Annie, and she flew at François, her fists pummelling his chest in her rage. 'How *dare* you!'

Laughing, François caught her hands and held them fast and, as she struggled to free herself, he said quietly, 'You're beautiful when you're angry, Annie.'

She was so surprised that she couldn't reply. He took one of her hands up to his lips and kissed it, then he released her and walked quickly away.

'I hate you!' she shouted after him.

Furious and confused, she headed for her cabin.

Chapter Four

As soon as Annie walked into the cabin, May, Andries and Susan all stopped talking and looked at her.

'What?' she said, frowning. 'What is it? What's happened?'

Her father was grinning broadly and he came forward and hugged her. 'We have some wonderful news,' he said.

She looked from one to the other. Susan was looking as happy as Andries. Only May looked glum.

'News?' repeated Annie.

Wonderful news? she thought. *What news on board ship could possibly be wonderful? Had Lucas, by some miracle, suddenly learnt the alphabet? Had the captain decided to double the crew's rations?*

Andries released Annie and went to Susan. He put

his arm round her shoulders. 'Your mother has just told us,' he said.

'What, Mother?'

May raised her eyes skywards. 'For heaven's sakes, Mistress Annie, for a girl who is supposed to be so well educated, you're very slow. Have you had your head in the clouds these past weeks? Did you not wonder why your mother was still feeling ill when the rest of us had long overcome our seasickness?'

Slowly, Annie turned to her mother. 'You're not . . . you're not with child, Mother?'

Susan nodded happily and stretched out her hand towards Annie. 'Yes, my love. I am to have another baby. After all this time I am to have another baby!'

Annie took her mother's hand and sat down abruptly on the edge of the bunk. 'I'm happy for you, Mother, but . . .'

Susan nodded. 'I know what you are thinking. What a time for it to happen, eh? For sure, it is far from ideal but, God willing, I shall be delivered of a healthy baby, despite our circumstances.'

Annie squeezed her mother's hand and suddenly all the changes, the emotions, the uncertainties of their situation overwhelmed her.

'There there, child, don't cry,' said Susan.

Annie sniffed and wiped her eyes with the back of her hand.

'I'm sorry, Mother. I'm happy for you, I really am.'

'Pray God the poor mite won't be born on board ship,' muttered May darkly.

'Oh no, there's no chance of that, May,' said Andries. 'We shall be in Java by the time the child is due. He will be born on dry land.'

He? thought Annie. *Why should her father assume that the child would be a boy? And to be born in the disease-ridden tropics! What were the chances of a newborn infant surviving there?*

The voyage continued and Annie started to implement her plan to make herself indispensible to Jacob. Every morning after prayers she stayed on the main deck and watched him tend the sick. As he had predicted, the further south they sailed and the warmer the weather became, so more and more crew members fell seriously ill and had to be treated below, so he had less time to give to those who were still on their feet.

One morning, Baernt was absent. 'Where's your assistant, Jacob?' asked Annie. Jacob looked up from dressing a wound. His face was pale and strained. 'Unwell,' he said shortly.

Annie said nothing but, with one eye on Jacob, she bent down and took a clean rag from the surgeon's box, then she approached the next man in line and started to undo his dressing. The man leered at her.

'There'll be more men up here if they know there's a pretty wench to tend to them,' he whispered, and although Annie winced at the stink of his fetid breath, she didn't move away.

Jacob looked up. 'What do you think you're doing, Annie?' he said.

Annie didn't answer and continued to unwind the man's bandage. For a moment, Jacob watched her silently. Then he sighed. 'All right, Annie, just for now, while Baernt is sick, but this is not to be a regular occurrence.'

'Of course not,' said Annie.

'That's a shame, sir,' said another man. 'We like the feminine touch, don't we, boys?' There was a murmur of assent and some ribald comments.

Jacob raised his voice. 'Silence! Let Mistress Annie get on with her work – or you'll have me to answer to.'

Annie smiled to herself. Jacob had said 'her work'.

Later, Annie approached her father and told him what she'd done. She didn't want him to hear it from anyone else and she didn't want to ask her mother's permission; Susan was sure to say no.

'Father, the surgeon's assistant is unwell and Jacob has no one to help him.'

Andries was leaning on the railing, staring out to sea, no doubt dreaming of their wonderful new life in the East. 'Oh, poor Jacob,' he said, vaguely. 'I'm sorry to hear that. I imagine his workload is burdensome in this heat.'

'So I've been helping him.'

Andries was suddenly alert. 'Helping him? In what way?'

'Just simple jobs, Father. Bandaging and suchlike.'

'You've not gone below?'

'Oh no, Father. I would never do that,' said Annie. 'I'm just helping him when he holds his sick parade on deck, after morning prayers.'

Andries frowned. 'You mother won't like it.'

'It's not for long, Father. Only until Jacob's assistant recovers.'

Sighing, Andries said, 'Oh, very well. I can see no harm in it. But you must be careful. The seamen and soldiers are a rough lot.'

'They may be rough, Father, but they need to be kept healthy for all our sakes.'

Andries looked at her. 'Umm, for sure, Annie, for sure. We all need to keep our health. We must reach Java in good health.'

Was it her imagination, or did her father say the word 'Java' with less enthusiasm than usual?

'What will it be like there, Father? For Mother and May and me?'

He looked surprised. 'For you? Well, I had not given

that much thought, but there will be other Company families there.'

Annie fought back her anger. Were they to see out their time in Java enclosed in the garrison, unable to go anywhere else, with only similarly marooned families for company? Why, in Zeeland there had at least always been plenty to do in their bustling town, and they never lacked for lively intercourse. She thought back to those she had left behind, to her friends and playmates, to the folk who came and went from their house, to the bustling markets and noisy streets, to the old tutor who had instructed her – until Father could no longer afford to pay him.

'But what shall I *do* there, Father?'

Andries smiled down at her. 'Do? Why no doubt there will be plenty of young Company men to charm.'

Annie stamped her foot in frustration. 'Father, I do not care to sit waiting for some Company man to pay me attention.' And, unbidden, the laughing face of François came into her mind's eye. 'Huh!' she said, then gathered up her skirts and walked away.

Baernt was not seriously ill and, in a day or two, he was back at his post, furious to find that Annie had replaced him in his absence and even more angry that Jacob did not dismiss her on his return.

Jacob had meant to. He'd had every intention of

dispensing with her services once Baernt had recovered. However, as the days went on, he began to rely on her. He could see that her skill was speeding things up and gradually he began to trust her and assign her more and more of the simple and less gory jobs such as applying ointment, redressing wounds or administering medicines under his instruction. He watched her closely but he could find no fault with her. She was as quick and skilful as Baernt was slow and clumsy.

Now that they were sailing down the west coast of Africa towards the tropics, poor Jacob was horribly overworked. One day, instead of rushing below after the morning sick parade, he stayed on deck and spoke to Annie.

'They've given me another man to help with the sick below,' he said. 'But he's as unskilled as Baernt and I spend all my time instructing him.' He sighed and wiped his brow with the back of his hand.

Annie looked at him. His face was drawn and his eyes restless – and he had lost weight.

'Jacob, please let me come and help you.'

He shook his head. 'No. The sights down there are not for a girl,' he said. 'You've no idea of the wretched state of some of the men.'

'Do they all have scurvy?'

He nodded. 'Many of them. And none will recover unless they have fresh food. Their symptoms are vile,

Annie. Rotting gums and rigidity. I would not like you to see such things. And malaria, too – the disease of the tropics – is taking its toll.' He paused. 'If they had been strong and well fed in the beginning, some may have avoided the scurvy, at least.'

The captain ordered the ship to be thoroughly cleaned and fumigated between decks, but still the death toll continued to rise. Annie lost count of the number of burials at sea.

There was a time, as they were sailing around the coast of Scotland through the treacherous North Sea, when they had cursed the storms and cold, but now, in the tropical heat, they had worse problems. Aside from the sickness on board, there was no wind to drive them forward. Day after day, they crawled along on a dead calm sea.

Everyone was bad-tempered, even Jacob. He had been so busy that he'd frequently missed his meals, and his presence at the captain's table became so rare that the day he did appear, he was greeted particularly warmly by the others. But when the talk turned to the sickness on board, he carefully put his glass of wine down on the table. Annie noticed how his hand shook as he did so.

'The condition of your men would be a deal better, Captain Wysvliet,' he said quietly, 'if you had not kept your crew on short rations for the whole of this voyage.

If they had eaten properly they would have been stronger to resist all this sickness.'

There was a stunned silence round the table and everyone except the captain and Annie avoided Jacob's blazing eyes. The captain's face was red with anger, and Jacob's was pale, and they glared at one another. Annie scraped back her chair and stood up, then she went to Jacob's side and took his arm. She could feel his body was trembling with rage.

'Annie, come and sit down at once,' said her father, but she ignored him. She stood at Jacob's side and addressed those seated at the table.

'None of you has any idea of how hard the master surgeon works,' she said, her voice shaking with the injustice of it all. 'Why, he hardly sleeps and he has no proper help. Those two assistants of his are slow and clumsy. Can't you see what his work means to him? He is killing himself with the effort of trying to save lives.'

They all looked at her in astonishment. Her father made to rise but Susan put a restraining hand on his arm. She cleared her throat.

'The master surgeon has been a good friend to our family,' she said.

Annie stared at her mother, usually so quiet and measured. Her words had calmed the explosive atmosphere and the other passengers began to add their comments, also praising the surgeon. The undermerchant and the preacher joined in and Annie could see the obvious discomfort of the other officers at the table at the temporary isolation of the captain.

Annie looked across at Captain Wysvliet, his face set in a scowl.

I'm not frightened of him any more, she thought. *I despise him.*

Meanwhile, Jacob had not moved. Annie shook his arm gently. 'Come, Jacob,' she said. 'You need to rest. Let me take you back to your cabin.'

'No,' said her father. 'You are not to go below, Annie.'

Susan spoke up again. 'I'm sure that the master surgeon will find a junior officer to escort her back,' she said.

To think that it is my mother who is encouraging me to venture below! Pregnancy must have softened her brain.

Suddenly the fight left Jacob and his shoulders sagged. He leaned on Annie's arm and together they left the cabin. When they reached the hatchway, he released her.

'I shouldn't have spoken in that way,' he said quietly. 'But thank you for supporting me, Annie. Now you should return to the captain's table.'

'No,' said Annie firmly. 'I'm coming down to the orlop deck with you.'

Jacob sighed. 'Oh, very well, Annie, you have worn

me down; and I'm too tired to resist you.'

She smiled, but a tiny lurch of fear gripped her. She had never heard Jacob admit weakness before.

With Jacob at her side, she had no fear of going below. A few crew members turned to look at them as they passed the gun deck, but none dared to make any comments and they reached the orlop deck without incident. However, as soon as they arrived, everyone was clamouring for Jacob's attention.

'There's another case of scurvy reported, Master Surgeon.'

'And a soldier with a high fever.'

Jacob stumbled towards his dispensary and started to get out medicines. Annie looked around her. No wonder the poor man was so exhausted. There were men lying on mattresses, groaning and thrashing about or lying horribly still. And his two assistants, it seemed, could do nothing without his instruction, for they only appeared when they heard his voice.

'Sir?' A weak cry came from one of the prone men. Annie looked at the speaker, then she turned quickly away, sickened by the sight.

'Yes? What is it, my friend?' asked Jacob, kneeling down beside him.

'I wish to make my will.'

Jacob sighed. 'Wait a little. When I have mixed these draughts and administered them, I'll attend to it.'

'Jacob?' whispered Annie. 'You surely could get someone else to witness his will?'

'It's not just the witnessing, Annie,' he said wearily. 'They can't write down their wishes, so they need a scribe. It is the least I can do for them when they are near death.'

'But what about one of the midshipmen? Could they not help?'

Jacob shrugged and turned back to his work. His eyes were glazed and he was moving jerkily, as if worked by some unseen puppet master. He seemed momentarily to have forgotten Annie and she stood among the sick and dying, overwhelmed by the hopelessness of it.

There was a noise behind her and someone came out of the midshipmen's quarters.

'I thought I heard your voice, Annie. What in God's name are you doing down here?'

She turned to see François at the door of his cabin and her temper flared. What right did he have to question her? She picked her way through the sick and went over to him, eyes blazing.

'Oh, for goodness' sake, François, stop being so infernally arrogant and look about you,' she whispered. 'Can you not see what is happening to Jacob? The strain on him is intolerable and I cannot see how he can continue to bear it.'

François frowned. He opened his mouth to say

something but thought better of it.

Annie stamped her foot. 'Why can't he have more help?'

There was an awkward silence between them as Annie glared at him and François looked over her shoulder towards the surgeon as he mixed up draughts in the dispensary.

'I know, Annie,' said François at last. 'The poor man is cruelly overworked.'

'Lord, François, you almost sound sincere. Where's the witty remark, the sarcastic quip?'

'Not this time,' he said, half smiling at the rebuke. 'Some situations don't merit such humour.'

Annie was momentarily disconcerted. She wasn't used to this sincere François. It didn't seem natural. She went on, tumbling over her words. 'And, on top of all his other duties, the poor man is writing wills for the dying. Surely someone else could take that burden from him?'

'We do help, when we can, Annie, but we have many other duties, as you know. And the dying won't wait at our convenience.'

She gave a faint smile.

François looked thoughtful. 'Perhaps it is something that you could do,' he said slowly.

'Me! How? How could I possibly do it? I'm not welcomed below decks, as you very well know. I only came now because poor Jacob made an outburst at the captain's table and . . . well, I prevailed upon him to let me escort him to his cabin.'

François raised his eyebrows. 'An outburst? What sort of outburst?'

'He accused the captain of keeping the crew on short rations and making them weak and susceptible to disease. And . . . and I supported him. And I'm glad I did. It is time that Wysvliet faced up to the consequences of his actions.'

'Fighting talk, Annie, but it won't change anything.'

Her eyes flashed. 'Well at least I spoke out!' she said. 'As did my mother and others. And who knows, he may *have* to change his ways if the passengers take him to task.'

'Huh!' said François. 'Nothing will change, you mark my words.'

The angry retort on Annie's lips was silenced by the sound of the ship's bell, signalling the change of watch.

François's head jerked up. 'This is my watch; I'm on duty. Now, are you going to spend the rest of the night here ranting, or shall I take you back to the upper decks?'

Annie turned her head away so François didn't see her smile. Damn the boy. How dare he make her smile when she felt so angry?

'I suppose I must go back,' she muttered and,

although she frowned when François took her arm, in truth she was glad of his presence as they passed the gun deck, and she glanced nervously at the men huddled there, some staring boldly at her.

Just before they reached her cabin, François stopped and stood looking down at her. 'You know, I admire you, Annie,' he said. 'Not many passengers bother themselves about the state of the crew, yet you are bandaging the sick, trying to teach that dunderhead of a ship's boy to read, and even feeding the wretched cat.'

Annie frowned. 'It fills the time,' she muttered. François released her arm. 'No,' he said slowly. 'It's more than that. You have a kind heart, Annie, underneath that fiery exterior.'

She bit back a snappy retort, lowered her head and ducked through her cabin door.

Chapter Five

For day after day the *Zuytdorp* lay near motionless on the flat sea and the sun beat down relentlessly on passengers and crew alike. The ship's progress was painfully slow, the water supply was getting low and it was rank and full of worms, but for the crew it was all there was to drink. The supplies of small beer had long since run out and the animals on board had all been eaten or died from other causes.

The passengers were listless. Even Andries's enthusiasm was waning, and he had stopped remarking on the strange fish they could see in the clear waters beneath them, some huge and flat, some with fins and others in great, constantly shifting shoals, the sun flashing on them as they turned this way and that. They even saw fish seemingly flying out of the water.

But all these wonders had lost their charm as they waited, listlessly, for some wind to fill the great sails of the *Zuytdorp* and move them on their way.

Then, on 8 October, there was a shout from one of the topmen.

'Clouds to starboard!'

Everyone who heard the shout stopped what they were doing and there was an expectant silence as they stood watching. It was as if the whole ship's company was holding its breath, praying for the clouds to come their way and disgorge some rain. During the next hour, as the clouds rolled closer and the sky darkened, Annie and May stood on deck, their eyes fixed on the sky.

'I never thought I'd pray for it to rain,' said May. 'Think of all that water in the canals at home and how we used to curse the dark wet days of winter.'

'We should pray for wind, too,' said Annie. 'Wind to fill the sails and get the ship moving again.'

The wind was imperceptible at first, but soon it began to strengthen and Annie untied her cap so that it could blow through her hair and give her some relief from the heat. As the wind grew still stronger and the first drops of rain began to fall, the deck suddenly became alive with activity. Sails were hoisted and containers placed on deck to catch the water and, as the great fat drops fell on them, Annie and May stood laughing, drenched in a tropical storm, delighting in the feel of the streams of water dousing their bodies.

For a blessed twenty-four hours, the ship made progress and tempers improved.

'Thank the Lord,' said Susan. 'I was beginning to think we were never going to move again.'

But her optimism was short lived and, when they awoke the next day, it was to the all too familiar blazing sun and dead calm sea.

The weeks dragged on and the situation remained unchanged. Occasionally they made a little progress, drifting this way and that, trying to catch even the faintest puff of wind. Rumours abounded that the ship was cursed, that the sails would never fill again, that the captain and officers were at their wits' end.

'This is a ship of death,' moaned May, wringing her hands. 'I wish we'd never set sail on her. What will become of us?'

'We shall be on the move again soon, you'll see,' said Annie, but although her words were brave, she wasn't as confident as she sounded – and her mother was becoming more and more anxious.

'Dear Lord, Annie, perhaps May was right. Perhaps this baby will be born on board after all.'

'Surely not, Mother. You still have months to go and we shall have reached Java by then.'

Andries, too, had lost the spring in his step and no

longer talked with such enthusiasm about the riches that awaited them in the East.

And the death toll continued to rise. Jacob was given more help but it was still not sufficient to keep up with the rampant sickness.

One day, François came to their cabin. Annie was alone inside. Her parents were on deck and May was nowhere to be seen.

'Annie,' said François, and for once his face was serious. 'The master surgeon has asked for your help.'

Annie immediately closed the book she was reading. 'Of course I'll help. What can I do?'

'I've persuaded him to let you write the wills for some of the sailors and soldiers. And if you agree, I'll take you down now.'

Annie stood up and smoothed down her skirt.

'I'll come at once,' said Annie. 'Is there parchment?'

'Aye. And quills. The materials are not the problem, Annie. What they lack is a scribe.'

'I should tell my father, perhaps?'

'I've already spoken to him. He has no objection.'

How things have changed, thought Annie. *In these desperate times, conventions are being readily laid aside.*

As they made their way to the orlop deck, François said, 'There is superstition and nervousness down below, Annie. They whisper among themselves and spread rumours; they see such sickness around them that they are all clamouring for their wills to be written. They are all convinced that they will die before we reach the Cape, let alone Java.'

'And are their fears justified? How bad is the situation, François? Shall we ever move again?'

He shrugged. 'It's pretty bad, Annie. At this rate, we may have to change course and put in to the African coast. The fresh victuals are all used up and those suffering from scurvy won't survive without them.'

'And is the same true on board the *Belvliet*?'

'I believe so. She is lying some way off but she, too, is becalmed and they also have rampant sickness on board.'

As they passed the gun deck, Annie saw that it was being cleaned and fumigated yet again. Lucas was among those scrubbing and sweeping and Annie glanced across at him.

François followed her gaze. 'How's your little ship's boy getting along with learning his letters?'

She bridled. 'My little ship's boy, as you call him, is making progress. And he tries hard to please.' Then she sighed. 'But it is more difficult to find a time to teach him since all the animals in his care have been slaughtered.'

When they reached the surgeon's cabin, François left them. Jacob greeted her warmly but Annie was shocked at the sight of him. She'd not seen him for a while; he had left her and his two assistants to deal with the walking sick for the last few days so that he could spend more time with his patients below and, even in that short time, he had become more gaunt and his face more strained. And there was a constant twitch in one eye that hadn't been there before.

'Thank you for coming, Annie. Let me show you the men who need your help.'

He walked her round the mattresses, pointing them out. 'There are more, of course, lying sick in their hammocks on the gun deck, but I shall deal with them. If you can see to the needs of these men here, it will help me greatly.'

Annie squatted beside a young seaman and she could see that he didn't have long to live. He was wasted and his limbs were rigid and, when he opened his mouth to whisper out his wishes, the stink from his breath and rotting gums made her recoil. She gritted her teeth and smiled at him. Faithfully, she listed his possessions:

A few pipes, some tobacco, a linen undershirt and underpants, a blue-striped undershirt and pants, a watchcoat, an old mattress, an old woollen shirt, an old linen shirt, two white shirts, a blue shirt, a pair of new shoes, a pair of old shoes, an old English bonnet, a handkerchief, a pair of scissors and a knife.

It took a long time to extract the information from him and to learn that he wished his possessions to be auctioned on board after his death and any money kept for his family in Holland. But once he had expressed his wishes and put his mark at the bottom of the parchment, he seemed happier.

Annie spent the rest of the day writing down the wishes of the sick and dying and, when François came off watch, he found her still crouched down, writing in her strong legible hand. He touched her shoulder.

'That's enough for today, Annie. You need to come up for air.'

Wearily, she got to her feet. 'They have so little,' she said to him. 'To think that a few clothes and a bit of tobacco are often all they have in the world.'

François nodded. 'I'll take you back now.'

By the end of October, nothing had changed. Then one morning, as Annie was finishing her duties at the masthead, she saw the ship's boat being lowered and the captain, the undermerchant and the uppersteersman climbing down the rope ladder after two oarsmen and getting into it. As soon as they were settled, the oarsmen pulled away.

'What's happening?' she asked Baernt. 'Where are those officers going?'

Baernt had still not forgiven her for easing herself into what he saw as his domain and he never passed up an opportunity to thwart her.

He shrugged. 'How should I know?'

But Annie and the rest of the passengers were not kept in ignorance for long. At dinner, the captain made an announcement.

'Our current situation cannot continue,' he announced. 'We have waited for weeks for a decent wind and we can wait no longer.'

'So, what are we to do?' asked Andries.

Wysvliet leaned back in his chair. 'We have had a meeting with the officers of the *Belvliet* and we have reached a decision.'

Everyone at the table looked at him.

'We are to change course and head towards the African coast. We shall make landfall on the island of São Tomé in the Gulf of Guinea where there is a settlement. God willing, we shall find fresh meat and vegetables there and the sick will become stronger.'

The *Zuytdorp* limped onwards in a different direction now, and the wisdom of heading for the African coast was a topic for hot dispute.

'It is madness,' said Andries. 'Our journey will be delayed even more. At this rate we won't reach the Cape before the end of the year.'

'But Father,' said Annie. 'Look at the state of us. We all need fresh victuals; perhaps our family might survive until we reach the Cape, but those poor souls with scurvy won't.'

She was worried about Lucas. Whenever she could, she smuggled some food to him but even so, she could see that he was much weaker than before and he had lost interest in learning his letters. Annie tried to cheer him up.

'Come on, Lucas,' she said. 'We'll soon be on dry land again and then you'll get stronger. And when we reach Java you'll be able to read and write.'

He looked down at the slate on which she had written some simple words and pushed it away from him. 'What's the point, Mistress Annie? What's the point of learning my letters? I shall be dead before long.'

'Nonsense,' said Annie harshly. 'You are not to speak like that, Lucas.'

Lucas didn't meet her eyes. He drew circles with his finger on the deck. 'You don't know what it's like on the gun deck,' he mumbled. 'No one believes we shall reach the Cape. The men say they've never seen the like of it. They've never been becalmed for so long and they've never been in a ship where there's so much sickness.'

A tiny lurch of dread cramped Annie's stomach.

'Of course we shall reach the Cape. The captain knows what he's doing.'

'They all speak ill of the captain on the lower decks,' muttered Lucas.

Annie's head jerked up and looked about her. 'Be

careful what you say, Lucas. That's mutinous talk,' she whispered.

Lucas didn't answer.

When she left Lucas, Annie stayed on the main deck for a while. She had been shocked by his words – and frightened, too. She was aware of the change of atmosphere on board. It had been a gradual, subtle change, but since they had been in the tropics, the crew had become sullen and there was a watchfulness and unease between the officers. There was less singing among the men, less joking, and the punishments had become harsher and more frequent; often Annie found herself treating the lashes on a starving crewman's back.

She had spoken to Jacob about this but he'd not been as shocked as she had thought he'd be.

He repeated the mantra she'd heard before. 'Discipline is essential, Annie.'

'But surely there are other ways, now the men are so weak?'

He'd shaken his head. 'It is what they understand. It is what they expect.'

Her relationship with Jacob was beginning to show signs of strain and she wished she could speak to him as easily as they'd spoken earlier in the voyage. Where once there had been a light in his eyes, now they were dead and hooded with fatigue, and he was so distracted that he hardly took any notice of her. Every time she expressed concern about his own health, he was brusque.

'How can I rest, Annie? I have too much work to do.'

'But Jacob, you'll kill yourself if you continue like this. Please . . .'

He'd turned on her impatiently then. 'I can trust no one else to deal with these gravely ill men, Annie. You and the others are relieving the pressure by treating the walking sick and I can ask you to do no more.'

But she wasn't so easily put off. 'At least tell me what to look for, Jacob, when we treat men on the deck. Then perhaps we could help them earlier.'

Jacob had wiped his sweating brow on his sleeve. 'Baernt knows what to look out for, and he then reports back to me.'

Annie had forced down her irritation. 'But you've never told *me*, Jacob.'

He'd looked up then, genuinely surprised. 'I told Baernt to make sure you were aware . . .'

Annie had said nothing, though she was seething. Eventually, Jacob had said wearily, 'You know the symptoms of scurvy.'

'Yes. But what of other diseases? What of malaria?'

'Malaria? Oh, fever, headache, muscle aches, tiredness, vomiting, diarrhoea.'

'And is there no cure?'

Jacob had sighed. 'There is some bark in the Americas which they say has properties that can cure malaria, but I have no supplies here. If the body is strong then it can combat the fever and will survive. But the disease often recurs.'

Annie dragged her thoughts back to the present as she continued to look out to sea where, it seemed to her, the very birds in the sky were limp and exhausted.

'Have you spied any land yet, Mistress Annie?'

Annie turned to smile at May as she came towards her. May had changed, too. She had lost her plumpness and she was no longer the talkative girl, full of shipboard gossip gleaned from Jan, her friend in the galley. She'd even stopped moaning about the wretchedness of their situation. It was as if the heat and the motionless water had seeped into her veins and sapped them of all their vitality.

Annie said nothing. What was there to say?

Then, at last, on 6 November, land was sighted and the whole ship's company seemed to let forth a collective sigh of relief as the news spread. Soon everyone aboard could just make out a large island, shimmering on the horizon. They had reached São Tomé!

'God be praised, soon we shall be on dry land again.'

'And there will be fresh food and water.'

When Annie next saw François, she asked him how long he thought it would be before they reached the island.

'You mustn't get too excited, Annie,' he said. 'We are still on a dead calm sea. You may be able to see land, but it will be weeks before we get there unless there is a decent wind.'

'Oh, surely not, François. Don't be so gloomy.'

'I'm being realistic,' he said.

'Huh!' said Annie, and she walked away.

But he was right. It was another six weeks before the *Zuytdorp* reached the island and, during that time, Annie turned sixteen; but no one marked the day.

Chapter Six

'Wake up, Annie!' It was Father, shaking her. 'Wake up, girl. Wake up, May. And you too, Susan. I've been on deck since dawn, and we are about to drop anchor.'

The old Andries was back; his voice full of excitement. Annie, May and Susan all dressed as quickly as they could and hurried up on deck. The island, which had been so tantalizingly distant for so long was now, at last, only a little way away. Annie and May hugged each other.

'It's so green,' laughed May.

'And high,' said Annie. 'Look at those mountains!'

Susan came and joined them. The baby was showing now and she walked slowly and carefully across the deck.

'How I long for a spell on land,' she said wearily.

Together they watched as the *Zuytdorp* came about and there was a cracking of the sails as they were hauled in before the crew dropped anchor in the deep water not far from shore.

Suddenly May let out a shriek and pointed towards the shallows. 'God in heaven, what is that?'

A huge creature, more than twice the size of a man, was swimming among the sea grass. It had a huge fat body, little flippers and a great ugly head.

Susan felt for Annie's hand.

Just at that moment, one of the seamen passed by. He stopped when he saw them pointing, put his hand to shade his eyes and called over one of his friends.

'A sea cow,' he said. 'I've heard tell of them but I've never seen one before. What a monstrous great creature it is.'

Annie squeezed her mother's hand. 'I don't think it can harm us, Mother,' she said.

They watched as it swam slowly along, keeping close to the shore, stopping every now and again to feed – then it disappeared round the headland.

May broke the silence. 'Pray God there aren't such creatures on land. When shall we go on shore?' she asked. 'Shall we go today?'

'No, May,' said Annie. 'The captain told us that it will be several days before we are allowed off the ship. The sick will go first, then the rest of the crew will clean the decks and then we'll leave before the ship is taken to the shore and turned on its side for repairs.'

'Still more time on board! How shall we bear it?'

'Just as we have borne it these last five months,' said Annie sharply.

May raised her eyes to the sky. 'May God give me patience, then,' she muttered.

For the next few days, they watched as the ship's boats went back and forth to the island, carrying essentials for setting up camp on the shore. Jacob was one of the first officers to go, accompanying the sick, together with a party of men to tend them.

Their sister ship, the *Belvliet*, also anchored off the island and started to disembark its sick. There was a rumour that their captain – Blaauw – was unwell himself.

Then, at last, the time came for the passengers and the rest of the crew to be taken ashore in the longboats. Susan was nervous going down the ladder and Andries had to hold on to her. Even so, she nearly lost her footing when she climbed into the boat as it bobbed in the azure sea. She was awkward with the bulk of the baby and her ankles were swollen, making her clumsy.

'Oh, Lord save me,' she cried as she slipped, but there were plenty of hands to help her and she sat down thankfully on the plank across the middle of the boat. Annie and May followed and everyone's spirits rose as they drew nearer the shore, but when, at last, they clambered out of the boat on to the sand, Annie and May lurched uncertainly on their feet.

'Gracious, Mistress Annie,' laughed May. 'We've been at sea so long we've forgotten how to walk on the land.'

'Aye,' said one of the seamen. 'You've still got your sea legs, now you must learn to change them for your land legs!'

On shore, already there was a large camp set up, with rough tents made from sailcloth for shelter. Annie and her family looked around them in amazement. The seamen and soldiers had been busy cleaning themselves up and there were garments drying on the canvas or spread over the undergrowth further up the beach.

'There must be plenty of fresh water, then,' said Susan, 'if they can wash their linen so freely.'

'Plenty,' said Andries. 'I'm told that there are a mass of streams crossing the island, coming down from the mountains.'

'Fresh water,' sighed May. 'I never valued it so highly as now.'

Annie looked round for the surgeon but couldn't see him. But she did see a lot of strangers – black men and women – walking in among the tents, fetching and carrying. She pointed them out to May.

'Lord!' said May, fearfully. 'Who are they?'

Andries overheard her. 'Slaves, from the mainland of Africa,' he said. 'When the Portuguese had the island, they captured blacks from the mainland to work on the sugar plantations they established here.'

'And for the slave ships that take them to the Americas,' added Susan.

'Aye, for that, too,' said Andries.

Annie was scared to see so many black faces at close quarters, but she felt sorry for them, also.

'But the island belongs to the Dutch now, does it not, Father? Do the Dutch ships take slaves to the Americas, too?'

'Yes, of course,' said Andries, but Annie could tell that the subject interested him little. 'I must go and find someone to show us to our quarters,' he added, and he walked off to talk to some of the officers.

Annie continued to stare at the blacks. Jacob had told her something of the slave trade – which he condemned as inhuman – and she was imagining what it must be like to be violently taken from your home and forced on to the slave ships, kept chained below decks in conditions even worse than those of the crew on board the *Zuytdorp* and then set to work in plantations in a foreign land where you had no rights.

A little later, Andries appeared with François and a couple of seamen.

'We are to be billeted in some comfort,' he said,

smiling. 'François and these two will show us where to go.'

The seamen shouldered the family's sea chest and their other possessions and they all followed François up the beach and on to a track. The foliage soon became dense on either side and full of the sound of birdsong. They saw the flash of small, brightly coloured birds as they darted from tree to tree. Once, May stopped in her tracks and pointed. 'Lord, what is that?' as a strange looking grey bird flew across their path.

'That's a parrot, miss,' said one of the seamen.

'Fancy,' said May. 'What a queer place this is.'

'A bit different from what we are used to in Zeeland, eh, May?' said Andries. 'And we shall see many more exotic sights when we are in Java, no doubt.'

Annie sighed and dropped back to be with her mother, who was finding it difficult to walk on the rough track in the heat and humidity. Father's humour had quite returned but it seemed to Annie that this journey would never end, that they would never reach Java. François was striding ahead and she watched as he spoke with her father. It occurred to her suddenly that she had never before seen him on dry land, and he seemed changed, a little, without the structure of shipboard life to sustain him. But maybe that was fanciful.

At last the track widened out into a huge clearing.

On slightly higher ground there was a settlement of sorts, with a large house at its centre and some buildings round about it and cultivated land beyond, stretching in all directions.

François pointed to the house. 'This is the old Portuguese settlement,' he said, 'but we own the island now, so the sugar plantations are overseen by the Dutch.'

Annie put her hand up to her eyes and squinted towards the fields. 'There's nothing to see in the fields,' she said.

'That's because the cane has all been harvested,' said François.

Annie said nothing but she felt stupid. *He doesn't know any more than I do,* she thought. *He will only just have been told that.*

Why did he always come over as so superior?

Their time at São Tomé was, on the whole, a happy one. They were made comfortable at the settlement and they were able to wash themselves and their clothes. And there was abundant fresh food and water. The jungle was full of exotic fruits and the sea was full of fish. There were no dangerous animals on the island but, despite this, the heat and humid atmosphere took its toll and there were more deaths. Although the surgeon urged everyone to cover their flesh as much as possible when they were outside, to avoid being bitten by insects or burned by the sun, many of the men took no notice and seemed to be permanently scratching themselves, their sunburnt skin a mass of bites.

For most of the time, Annie and May kept to the settlement and its surroundings, but occasionally the family would venture down the track to the sea's edge. On one of these trips, Annie spotted Lucas returning, with some others, from an expedition to fetch firewood. She waited until he was away from the group and then she approached him.

'Are you being kept busy, Lucas?' He smiled at her and she saw how he had changed. Washed clean, and with better food, he was no longer the stinking, starving, sore-ridden boy, but quite a pleasant looking lad. He had even washed his hair and, instead of resembling mouldy hay, it was fair and untangled.

'Aye, Mistress Annie. There's plenty to do.'

'Not too busy to keep up with your letters, I hope.'

Lucas hung his head and said nothing. Annie clicked her tongue. 'Then I shall give you a lesson now.'

'But, Mistress Annie, there are no materials . . .' he began.

She laughed. 'Look at your feet, Lucas. We can write in the sand.'

While Annie was instructing a reluctant Lucas, May went in search of her friend Jan and, on her return, she was gloomy.

'What's the matter, May? He hasn't fallen out of love with you, has he?'

May sat beside them on the sand. 'No, Mistress Annie. At least I don't think so. But he is in a bad humour.'

'Why is that?'

'Because two of his helpers have died and he will have too much work to do once we go back on board.'

Annie shrugged and didn't answer. She was well used to May's tales of woe – and besides, she had seen François coming over to speak to her. May nudged her in the ribs and, as he approached, she found herself blushing.

'Still persevering with your pupil then, Annie?' said François, smiling down at the two of them, but he only paused briefly before walking off.

Annie was irritated that he hadn't stopped – and angry with herself that she felt so disappointed. When she released Lucas from making his letters in the sand, she went looking for the surgeon. She had hardly seen him since being on the island; he had elected to stay at the camp and not to sleep in more comfort in the house. When she found him, he was sitting in his makeshift dispensary, reading.

'How are your patients, Jacob?'

He started and then looked round at her. 'Ah,

Annie, I was deep in my studies,' he said. Then he closed his book and gave her his full attention. 'Well, we have had many more deaths, as you know, because of this wretched climate.'

'But some of the scurvy patients are recovering, are they not, Jacob?'

He smiled briefly. 'Yes, yes, those who weren't too far gone or who have not succumbed to other disease – they are recovering. It is a wonder what fresh fruit and vegetables will do for them.'

A couple of weeks after this, the captains of the two ships declared that the *Zuytdorp* and the *Belvliet* were repaired and cleaned and ready to sail again. There was a great deal of activity, then, as boatloads of firewood were taken on board together with barrels of fresh water, ten cows, and fresh fruit and vegetables. There was such a bustle and crowding as the two ships were loaded that it was not until everyone was back on board the *Zuytdorp* that a head count was made and it was discovered that eight members of the crew were missing. Andries reported this to his family.

He listed them on his fingers. 'A topman, a cabin boy, a carpenter, two soldiers, two seamen and a cook.'

May looked up sharply. 'A cook?' she said. 'Do you know his name?'

Andries shook his head. May stood up and rushed

out of the cabin.

'What's the matter with her?' asked Andries.

Annie shrugged. She was not about to tell her parents about May's romance with Jan.

'What will happen, Father? Will they search the island?'

Andries shook his head. 'No. The captain does not wish to delay any further. And in any case,' he said, 'the island is so thick with jungle that it would take days to track them down.'

Poor May, thought Annie. *Pray God it's not Jan.*

A little later she went up on deck to look for May and she found her huddled outside the galley, crying. Annie sat down beside her. 'Was it Jan who deserted?' she asked.

May looked up at her, red-eyed. 'Yes,' she said, sniffing. 'The bastard! How could he say all those things to me and then leave me like this?'

Annie put out her hand and stroked May's face. 'I'm so sorry, May,' she said.

May sniffed again. 'I thought he was up to something,' she said quietly. 'You remember I told you of his bad humour?' Annie nodded. 'Well,' May went on, 'I reckon he'd been planning it a long time – him and them others.' She looked down at her feet. 'He told me once that he was sure that this ship was doomed, that it would never make it to Java.'

'Then he was filling your head with nonsense,' said Annie sharply. 'Of course we shall reach Java.'

On 3 January 1712, the *Zuytdorp* and the *Belvliet* weighed anchor and sailed away from the island. They made one more brief stop beside the African coast to pick up some more supplies, and then on 16 January they sailed for the Cape. The weeks went by with the routines unbroken. Jacob fell into a deep depression as the death toll continued to rise and he was powerless to prevent it. Annie tried to help when she could, but Baernt blocked her at every turn and Jacob seemed too listless to defend her.

One evening, as Annie was coming out of the captain's cabin after dinner, Jacob was waiting for her.

'Jacob!' she said. 'I'm so pleased to see you. Have you come to ask me to help?'

Jacob stared at her. His eyes were sunk deep into their sockets and his cheeks were hollow. He shook his head impatiently and Annie noticed that the nervous twitch in his eye had returned. She put her hand on his arm. 'Jacob, you're not well,' she said.

He shrugged and then he cleared his throat and his voice was thin and rasping. 'I've come to bring you something, Annie,' he said and, with trembling hands, he reached into the pocket of his jacket and drew out a pouch, which he handed to her.

Annie loosened the strings at the top of the pouch and took out an engraved silver tobacco box.

'It's beautiful, Jacob, but it's yours. I've so often seen you use this box. You should not give it away.'

He shook his head again. 'I would like you to have it, Annie. Please . . .'

And then he was gone, stumbling back to the hatch to go down to the orlop deck.

She puzzled over the incident and she found it hard to sleep that night.

The next morning, at prayers, there was disquiet among the crew and the officers. Something had happened, she could sense it. And then, when the preacher started to pray for Jacob's soul, her worst fears were confirmed. As soon as prayers were finished, she rushed over to Baernt, at the masthead.

'Baernt! What's happened? For God's sake, tell me.'

Baernt turned to her. 'Jumped overboard,' he said harshly. 'During the first watch.'

Annie turned away, sickened by his callousness. Later, she learnt that the seamen had seen Jacob too late and had been unable to stop him. Miserably, she went back to the cabin and took out the tobacco box from its pouch. She opened up the lid. There, lying inside the box, was a note, tightly folded. She smoothed it out and read the wobbly writing.

God bless you, Annie. And beneath was written Jacob Hendricx.

Annie held the note to her lips and kissed it, her eyes filling with tears.

'Jacob, why did you do this? No one could have done more for the people on this ship. Why did you torture yourself so?'

Then she carefully replaced the note inside the box and put the box back in the pouch and tied the strings in a knot so that she could slip it around her neck. She touched it at her throat.

'I'll always wear it like this, Jacob. I'll never forget you.'

Chapter Seven

The surgeon's death had unsettled them all, especially Annie and her family. 'Lord, Andries,' said Susan. 'What will happen to the sick with no surgeon on board?'

'We shall be at the Cape soon, Susan. They will take on a new surgeon at the Cape, for sure.'

Nothing on this voyage is sure, thought Annie.

Annie's night-time prayers were longer now. She prayed that her family would survive the voyage, that her mother would be safely delivered of her baby; and she always prayed for the soul of Jacob, weeping silently as she held on to the pouch which was always at her neck.

You were a saint, Jacob. You are surely in heaven and at peace now – but why did you have to desert us?

In her heart, though, she knew the reason. The strain he had endured had affected his mind and he, of all people, would have recognized this. A surgeon with shaking hands and of unsound mind would be a danger to his patients.

Although there were more fresh victuals, the crew were still kept on short rations and the atmosphere on board was far from happy. Lucas was back on the quarterdeck, tending the cows from the island, so Annie could trap him there and continue to teach him his letters. She had more time on her hands, now, for Baernt refused to let her near the sick, either on the main deck or below.

'It's so wrong,' she said to May one day. 'I am better than him and those other heavy-handed men who help him. He has no knowledge of medicines and at least I have a little; the surgeon used to explain to me what he was doing. And more men are dying because Baernt and the others don't care.'

'No chance of *him* throwing himself overboard, I suppose?' said May. She was gloomy company these days and would talk of little else except the treachery of men in general and Jan in particular.

Annie and her family spent most of their time on deck now. They were no longer becalmed but the winds were fickle and contrary and the ship often had to tack this way and that to catch the breeze.

'I've been speaking with the captain,' said Andries one day, coming to them in high excitement. 'We've lost the *Belvliet*.'

Annie looked up, startled. 'Lost the *Belvliet*? What do you mean, Father?'

'It's these damned difficult winds,' he said. 'Both ships have had to go well off course to make progress, and now we've lost sight of our sister ship.'

'Is that so bad?' asked Annie.

'Of course it is bad. Why do you think we have a sister ship? It is so that we can keep in touch with each other so that if any accident befalls one, the other can come to its rescue.'

'More bad news,' muttered May.

Annie felt for the pouch hanging around her neck. They would be on their own, now, sailing down to the Cape, with no backup if they hit storms or had other misfortunes.

'I don't like it,' said May. 'All alone on this ocean, in this floating coffin. How many more poor souls will die before we reach the Cape?'

Andries turned away. For once he could think of no cheerful reply.

They ploughed on south towards the Cape. On some days they made good progress, but on others they had to tack across the ocean in pursuit of the elusive wind.

Anxiety had begun to affect them all. When they had set out from Zeeland, they had been told that they would reach the Cape of Good Hope in four months – five at most. But when, at last, they sailed into Table Bay at the Cape, on 23 March 1712, they had been at sea for eight months and, of the 286 originally on board, only 166 were left alive – 158 crew and eight passengers. And among those, twenty-two people were gravely ill.

Annie and her family were on deck when the *Zuytdorp* finally sailed majestically into Table Bay, and for once they felt proud of their magnificent ship, so much bigger than the others lying at anchor – but even the *Zuytdorp* was dwarfed by the mountain that towered above the garrison.

'Table Mountain,' said Susan. 'You can see why it is so called.'

Annie gazed at the flat topped mountain with its cloth of white puffy clouds. 'Yes,' she said. 'It's a good name for it.'

'Why are there so many ships in the bay?' asked May, her eyes wide.

'This is the main garrison of the VOC,' said Andries. 'This is the place where all the ships going to and from the East Indies stop off to reprovision. It's where the Company's storehouses are.'

'Shall we take on more crew, Father?' asked Annie.

'I imagine so.'

'And where will they come from?'

Her father shrugged. 'I expect they'll be recruited from the garrison and from some of the ships here in the bay.'

May's ears pricked up at the thought of new recruits. She nudged Annie and whispered, 'It will be good to have some new blood on board. I am heartily sick of all the old specimens.'

Annie raised her eyes to the sky and didn't reply.

There was a lot of activity during the next few days. The ship was cleaned again and more repairs undertaken. Then, one morning, Annie saw the captain and some of the officers being taken in the longboat over to one of the ships lying at anchor in the bay. By straining her eyes, she could just make out its name – the *Oostersteyn*. She also noticed that François was in the boat.

Much later in the day she spotted François standing on the quarterdeck, leaning on the rail and staring out to sea. She looked up at him and for once she was able to do so unobserved. He was a good looking boy, no doubt of that. She frowned. No – he was no longer a boy; this journey had changed him, as it had changed them all. Suddenly she found herself smiling as she took in his fair complexion and strong body. It was no longer the body of a youth but that of a man.

He turned suddenly and saw her and her heart missed a beat as their eyes met.

Stop it! she told herself and turned and walked casually away. But he bounded down the ladder.

When he reached her side she turned slowly to look at him, cursing herself for blushing. How could she not have noticed the change in him? How much older he looked now, no longer that fresh-faced, arrogant boy who she had so detested in the early weeks of the voyage. And, like all of them, his enthusiasm for the journey ahead seemed dulled – she had noticed that he no longer talked excitedly of Java and the promised riches it held.

He took her hand. Annie's blush deepened and she bit her lip. 'François, don't.' But she didn't withdraw it.

He smiled and said softly, 'And do you mind, Mistress Annie, if I hold your hand?'

She frowned and changed the subject. 'Why did the longboat go over to the *Oostersteyn* this morning?' she asked.

He moved closer. 'Nothing escapes your notice, does it, Annie? Well, I'll tell you, since I know you'll pester me if I don't; the captain of the *Oostersteyn* has conditionally agreed to transfer some of his crew to the *Zuytdorp*,' he said.

'Conditionally?'

François nodded. 'Yes,' he said thoughtfully. 'Our captain had a difficult time of it. The captain of the *Oostersteyn* is well known for taking particular care of his men and he wanted to be certain that Wysvliet will treat them well.'

'So, what conditions did he lay down?' asked Annie.

'Well, he'd heard how long we had taken to get here and he questioned Wysvliet closely about whether the supply of victuals had lasted.'

'Ah. And what did our captain say?'

'He boasted that he had had plenty of victuals and had only needed to take on fresh meat and vegetables. He even said he had enough stores to last us until we reached Java.'

'And the other captain believed him?'

'He looked astonished. And then he became angry and accused Wysvliet of keeping the crew short; his exact words were "Then you have denied or stolen food from your people."'

'And what did Wysvliet say to that?'

'He blustered a bit but in the end he had to admit that he'd kept the crew on short rations. *And* he had to agree to take on extra provisions here at the Cape, otherwise he wouldn't be supplied with the men from the *Oostersteyn*.'

'Do you think our captain'll stick to the agreement?'

François grinned. 'If he wants the extra crew, he'll

have to. The captain of the *Oostersteyn* won't keep the knowledge of Wysvliet's meanness to himself; and he has insisted on inspecting the provisions in our hold before he'll let any of his men on board the *Zuytdorp*.'

'He sounds to be a good and considerate man,' said Annie thoughtfully. 'Better than our captain, with his plans to starve his crew and line his own pockets.'

'I'll pretend I didn't hear that,' said François.

Annie looked up at him. 'But you must feel that, François? You can't respect a man like that.'

François looked serious for a moment. 'I'm a lowly midshipman, Annie. I have to respect the captain under whom I serve. That is naval law.'

'Hmm,' said Annie, withdrawing her hand gently from his. Then she grinned at him. 'I'm glad you're calling yourself lowly now!' And she ran swiftly down to the main deck before he could reply.

During the next few days Captain Wysvliet was forced to take on further supplies to obtain the new crew members from the *Oostersteyn*. Annie watched as live sheep, preserved meat, beans, peas, rice, water and fresh vegetables were all brought on board. But this did nothing to improve the captain's temper and the remaining passengers kept out of his way as much as possible.

'He's brooding on all the money he's had to spend,'

said May, when she and Annie passed him one day, scowling at the men loading more barrels.

'Well at least the crew will be better fed on the next leg of our journey,' said Annie, thinking of Lucas's scrawny frame.

Not long after this, their sister ship, the *Belvliet*, sailed into the bay, and there was general rejoicing on board the *Zuytdorp*.

'Thank the Lord she is safe.'

'We thought she may be lost.'

But their joy at seeing their sister ship sail safely into harbour was tinged with sadness. At dinner that night, Wysvliet told them that the *Belvliet*'s captain, Captain Blaauw, had died in the tropics.

Wysvliet has lost his co-conspirator, thought Annie.

By mid-April 1712, the *Zuytdorp* was ready to set sail again but, once more, the winds were contrary, so they didn't depart until 22 April, this time in the company of a much smaller ship, the *Kockenge*. However, they'd only been at sea for a few days when it became obvious that the *Zuytdorp* was a much faster vessel and, because it was getting late in the season and the captain wanted to make up some time, the *Zuytdorp* pulled ahead of the *Kockenge* and soon lost sight of her. Once again, they were alone on the ocean.

May's spirits were quite revived at the sight of so

many new crewmen, and even those who had been on board from the start of the voyage were well rested and already looking healthier. But there was one young German soldier, Michel Swarts, who had come on board at the Cape, whose presence made Annie feel uncomfortable. From the moment he had arrived, he had noticed her and she him. He had given her a bold look and then turned to his companion and muttered something and they had both laughed. Annie vowed to keep well out of his way, but he always seemed to be around and he made her feel uneasy.

There was, too, a new surgeon on board, but he was very different from Jacob. Annie had approached him to ask if she could help him but he had refused her offer.

'No, I thank you, mistress, I won't have women around the sick.'

Baernt, of course, was close by and couldn't conceal a satisfied smirk. So, once again, Annie had to content herself with teaching Lucas, reading and doing her needlework.

Susan was aware of her mood. 'I know you miss Jacob, Annie. Lord, we all do; he was a marvellous man – and so kind. But, God willing, you will soon have a little brother or sister to care for, and none of us will be idle then.'

Annie looked up from her needlework and smiled.

Susan's belly was large and swollen. 'It won't be long now, Mother, will it?'

Susan shook her head. 'Just a few more weeks. Though, I must confess, Annie, it worries me that I shall have the babe on board ship. It is no place to give birth.'

'I'll look after you, Mother.'

Susan reached out her hand and stroked Annie's cheek. 'You're a good girl, Annie. God bless you.'

But Annie was secretly terrified at the thought of helping her mother at the birth.

Despite the sadness and loss of life endured on board the *Zuytdorp*, now that the ship was reprovisioned and remanned, it was undoubtedly a happier place. The captain sailed south from the Cape and then due east.

'It's the better route,' said Andries, confidently. 'Apparently, when we head east we shall be blown across the ocean by the trade winds – the roaring forties.'

But Annie had heard mumblings among some of the older sailors about the proposed route.

'It is too late in the season to take this route, you mark my words.'

'Aye, there'll be winter storms when we sail north again alongside the unknown land.'

Winter storms? thought Annie. She couldn't

understand what they meant. It was the month of May – springtime. Surely they would be in Java long before winter?

She asked François what it meant and he became all superior.

'Silly girl,' he said. 'Don't you realize that we are going to the other side of the world? When it is summer in Zeeland, the weather on the other side of the world is in winter.'

Annie frowned, feeling foolish and ignorant, but she went on, 'Is it true, though, what the sailors are saying about storms off the coast of the unknown land?'

François adjusted a button on his jacket. 'There's always the possibility of winter storms,' he said.

'Oh, for heaven's sake, François,' said Annie, irritated again by his lofty ways. 'You don't know any more than I do. You've never been to the East before. I don't know why I bother asking you.'

She'd run off, then, cross that he had put her down in such a way. And angry, too, that she should bother about what he thought of her ignorance. Why should she be expected to know anything of winds and storms and suchlike?

Her worries were allayed when at last the ship turned and they were heading east. The winds were constant, the sails filled and they sped across the water.

And it was just at this moment, when all seemed

set fair at last, that Andries became sick.

At first, he refused to acknowledge that he was unwell, but Annie noticed he had lost his appetite and then that he was both shivering and sweating. Eventually, he could pretend no longer and he took to the cabin. The new surgeon was sent for.

Annie had seen plenty of cases of malaria when she'd visited the orlop deck and she told the new surgeon of her suspicions.

'I think I'll make the diagnosis, Mistress Annie,' he said sharply, ordering her out of the cabin.

Furious, she waited outside and, when the surgeon reappeared, she blocked his way. 'Well? Is it as I suspected?' she asked.

'Yes,' he said shortly. 'Your father has malaria and I have given your mother instructions for his nursing. I will visit each day.'

Annie watched him walk off. No sympathy, no kind words. So unlike Jacob.

She went back into the cabin to find her mother weeping. 'Oh, Annie,' she said, clutching at her. 'I'm so afraid. I have never seen him so unwell.'

Annie stroked her mother's hand. 'I can nurse him, Mother. Jacob told me what to do. And you mustn't distress yourself. Think of the baby and try to keep calm for its sake.'

Susan nodded. 'You are my rock, Annie. I thank

God every day that you are my daughter.'

Annie blushed. It was unlike Susan to compliment her.

For the next few days, Susan and Annie hardly left Andries's side and May, for once, acted the devoted servant, fetching clean linen to replace the sweat drenched undershirts, damp cloths for soothing Andries's fevered brow and thin soups to tempt him to eat. She took out the chamber pot without a grumble and made the cabin sweet smelling again with rags soaked in vinegar.

Once, when his temperature fell, he seemed to rally and he spoke to Annie, his voice a hoarse whisper. 'Look after your mother, Annie,' he kept repeating. 'If I die, swear to me you will look after your mother.'

Annie wiped his forehead. 'What's all this talk of dying, Father? The fever has left you. You will get better now.'

But Andries held her arm. 'Swear to me, Annie.'

Annie's eyes filled with tears. 'Of course I'll look after her, Father,' she said softly. 'Whatever happens, I shall do that.'

The next time the surgeon visited the cabin, Annie refused to leave her father's side. Eventually, the man gave in and shrugged his shoulders when Susan took him to task. 'Master Surgeon,' she said. 'My daughter has nursed her father with devotion, and she knows more than the rest of us of his disease. Why, our last surgeon trusted her to minister to the sick and explained symptoms and treatment to her.'

Annie looked gratefully at her mother, surprised that she should defend her in such a spirited fashion.

'Oh, very well,' said the surgeon. 'Stay if you must.' But when he had finished examining her father he addressed his remarks to Susan. 'As you can see, the fever has broken.'

'Thank God,' murmured Susan.

The surgeon cleared his throat. 'However,' he said, 'it often happens that the fever passes for a while, and then it returns.'

'But he will survive, will he not?' asked Susan.

The surgeon didn't answer at once. 'That depends, madam, on whether his body can resist another bout.'

Annie looked at Andries's wasted frame. Where had her robust father gone? In a matter of weeks the flesh had fallen off him and his eyes had sunken into their sockets. But, for the moment, he was lucid, and she tried to act normally and ignore her fear.

Even May was uncharacteristically tactful. She, like Annie and her mother, was wondering what would happen to them if Andries did not survive. Please God, this would not happen, but if it did, what then? When they reached Java, would they be sent back on another VOC ship?

But none of the women voiced their fears, even to one another.

And then, just as they had started to dare to hope again, when Andries's temperature had been near normal for three days, the fever gripped him once more.

And that night, Susan's pains began.

Chapter Eight

She had been suffering birth pangs for some hours and had managed to conceal the fact from Annie and May, but as the contractions became stronger, she couldn't control herself and she let out a long groan.

Annie left her father's side and went to her mother. 'Mother, what is it?'

'The baby's coming, Annie,' she whispered. 'Can you fetch clean linen and water?'

For a moment, Annie felt herself in the grip of terror. Her father was gravely ill, and now her mother was about to give birth and might not survive the ordeal. Childbirth, at the best of times, could kill the mother and now, in these conditions, the risks were high. She fought down her panic. She turned to May. 'Fresh linen and water, May,' but May was already on her way to fetch them. As another contraction ripped through her body, Susan gripped Annie's hand with such force that Annie felt her bones might break.

When May returned with the linen and water, Annie turned to her. 'May,' she said, as calmly as she could. 'Please sit by my father and continue to wipe his forehead.' She glanced towards May who, without her usual complaining, moved over to be near Andries.

'Don't fret, Mistress Annie,' said May. 'I'll help you with the birth. I've seen a good many babies brought into the world. I won't swoon.'

Annie smiled. 'Thank you, May,' she said quietly.

And so, as the day wore on and the afternoon turned into evening and they lit the lantern which hung on a beam above them, Annie and May struggled with life and death in their tiny cabin. At last, Susan's urge to push came over her and she cried out:

'The baby's coming.'

May turned and bent over Susan. 'I'm here, mistress. Keep pushing.' Then, a little later, 'I can see the head . . . you're nearly there.'

Annie stood to one side, grateful that May was taking over. Suddenly May was the capable one, unfazed by the mess of childbirth, her strong hands under the tiny, slippery head.

'One more push, mistress.'

Susan gave an animal cry and suddenly the rest of

the baby slipped out into May's hands. There was a moment's silence and then an indignant and lusty cry filled the cabin.

'A fine boy,' said May, holding the little bloodied scrap up to Susan.

'Oh, thank God,' gasped Susan, stretching her arms out for him.

Annie looked at her mother's face, which was transformed with happiness, and suddenly all the fatigue and worry overwhelmed her and she started to sob. Susan patted her hand.

'Don't cry, Annie,' she said gently. 'See, he's a strong boy. He will thrive, I am sure of it.'

Annie didn't trust herself to speak. Very carefully she touched the baby's palm and watched as his tiny hand curled around her finger. She felt then such love and protectiveness as she had never felt before. *Yes – you will thrive, little boy*, she thought, *because I will make sure of it. I swear to you that I will protect you until I have no more breath in my body.*

May's voice brought her back to earth. 'Why don't you go and tend your father, Mistress Annie? I'll get your mother and baby brother cleaned up.'

Brother! In all the time of her mother's pregnancy, Annie had never thought of the baby inside her mother as a real person. 'A brother,' she said to herself. 'I have a brother!'

Reluctantly, Annie withdrew her finger from the baby's grasp and went to be with her father. He was hardly conscious now, muttering occasionally and turning his head this way and that. Annie put her hand to his sweating forehead and felt the fierce heat.

'Father,' she said, taking his hand and squeezing it. 'Father, you have a son.'

But he didn't react. She looked over at May and her mother. May was bundling up soiled linen and helping Susan to wash both herself and the baby.

'Leave me be, May. I must let Andries see the baby now,' said Susan. There was a steeliness in her voice that frightened Annie. Why was her mother so determined to show the baby to his father before either of them were properly cleaned?

May put a restraining hand on her arm. 'No, mistress, you're too weak. Wait a while.'

But Susan took no notice. She heaved herself out of her bunk and, clutching the baby to her breast, staggered over to her husband's side.

'Andries,' she said, shaking his shoulder. 'Andries, look!'

Again, Andries didn't react, so Susan shouted at him.

'Look, man! For God's sake, look on your son. How many times have you said how you yearned for a son? We have one now, Andries, and he will live and be strong so that you can be proud of him. You must fight, Andries, fight for his sake! You must get better for his sake.'

Hearing the pride and desperation in her mother's voice, Annie should have felt some hurt, but she couldn't find it in her heart to be jealous of the tiny new life who, hearing his mother's raised voice, began to yell in earnest.

And it was then that Andries's eyes flickered open. Susan and the baby were only inches from his face. Just for a moment, he registered their presence and his mouth quivered into the ghost of a smile.

'A son,' he whispered.

'Aye,' said Susan, much more quietly. 'God has blessed us with a son.' Then she added, 'And he will be called after his father, as we had always intended.'

By this time, Annie was beside them and she saw her father's face relax as his head rolled to one side.

Susan looked at her, tears streaming down her face. Wordlessly, she handed the baby to Annie and leaned over her husband, cradling his head in her hands.

'Please don't leave us, Andries,' she whispered. 'Please keep fighting.'

She was shaking him again, trying to get a reaction, but his mouth was slack and his eyes closed.

Annie stepped away. The baby was still crying, his little face screwed up and his lips searching for food.

'Mother,' she said. 'I think the baby's hungry.'

But Susan didn't even look round. She continued to shake her husband.

'Please, Andries. Please wake up.'

Slowly, May came over. She leaned over Andries, her head close to Susan's, and gently put her finger on his neck. Then she straightened up. 'It's no good shaking him, mistress,' she said quietly.

Susan looked up sharply. 'What do you mean?'

May put a hand on Susan's arm. 'There's no pulse, mistress,' she said. 'He's gone. And all the shaking in the world won't bring him back to life.'

Susan continued to stare at her. 'No,' she said sharply. 'No, you're wrong, May. He's just unconscious.'

May shook her head. 'I've seen death before, mistress,' she said quietly.

Susan began to moan softly, never leaving go of Andries's head.

Annie looked at May. No words passed between them but both knew what the other was thinking.

What will happen to us now? Will we be abandoned in Java? Will the Company insist we travel back to Zeeland on another ship, to endure another nightmare journey? And will the baby survive?

Annie felt numb. It was too overwhelming. She stood there, first staring down at the baby squirming in her arms, then across at her mother, who was still rocking to and fro, her husband's head cradled in her hands, moaning.

'What shall we do, May? What will become of us?'

'Don't you go all weak, now, Mistress Annie. You're the strong one, remember?'

'But May . . .'

May sighed and squared her shoulders. 'Give me the baby,' she said. 'He needs to suckle.'

Annie handed him over and May took him to Susan.

'You must think of the living now, mistress,' she said. 'Your son needs to suckle.'

Susan looked up, her eyes wet with tears. Gently, she took the baby and put him to her breast.

Suddenly there was silence in the cabin.

'Come, mistress,' said May. 'Let me help you to your bunk.' Then she turned to Annie. 'You'd better tell the surgeon and the captain what has happened, Mistress Annie,' she said.

Annie looked down at her father. May was right. Annie, too, had seen death before, when she was helping Jacob, and she knew that her father was beyond help. His muscles were relaxed, his face at peace. There was no more fighting, no more pain.

She turned away at last. 'Yes,' she said quietly. 'Yes, you're right, May. I'll go and tell them now.'

She should have gone straight away to inform the captain, but as she walked out of the cabin she made her way slowly to the hatchway which led to the lower decks. She was so full of conflicting emotions that she hardly heard the lewd comments as she passed the gun deck on her way to the orlop deck to find the surgeon. Then, suddenly, she became aware of someone close behind her and, as she reached the great bulk of the mast just before she turned to climb down through the next hatchway, her way was blocked.

Grief lent an edge of steel to her voice. 'Let me pass,' she said.

But the man didn't move. 'Asking for it, ain't you, you saucy wench,' he whispered, his breath stinking, 'coming down here to tempt us.'

She recognized him then. It was the German soldier, Michel Swarts, the man who had joined the crew at the Cape and who had often muttered lewd comments or leered at her.

He didn't move and when she tried to push past him she felt his hand on her breast, tearing at the fabric of her dress. Something May had told her suddenly flashed into her brain and she poked a finger into the soldier's eye as hard as she could. He reeled back, yelling with pain, and Annie kicked out at him, freeing herself, then she ran, stooping low, tripping over her feet in her hurry, falling, scrabbling her way to the orlop deck where she knew her attacker would not follow. She kept running and didn't stop until she reached the midshipmen's cabin.

Oh God, François, be there. Please God let him be there, she thought as she wrestled with the door.

François was alone in the cabin and he jumped to his feet, startled, as she burst in.

'Lord, Annie, this is very forward of you . . .' he began. But then the smile froze on his lips and his tone changed as he saw her face, the tears streaming down her cheeks.

He came forward and put his hands on her shoulders. 'What's happened?'

She drew away from him and tried to control her sobs.

'Annie, you're shaking. Here, come and sit down.' He led her over to his bunk, and it was then that he noticed her torn dress and he took in the situation in a flash. His fist clenched. 'Who did this?' he asked quietly.

She shook her head. However much she was revolted by the attack, even in her distressed state, she knew what would happen to Michel Swarts if she reported him. She had no desire to see the flesh whipped off his back.

'Tell me!' insisted François, his voice rising.

Again, she shook her head, her sobs gradually subsiding.

'I am safe, François,' she said gently. 'I am safe now

– and I came down here on a more important errand.' She took a deep breath and it was some moments before she could bring herself to say the words. 'My father is dead,' she whispered at last. 'And my mother is delivered of a baby boy.'

François knelt on the cabin floor in front of her and took her hands in his.

'My God, Annie, I'm so sorry about your father. He was a fine man.'

'Aye,' she said, trying not to start crying again. 'Aye, he was.'

Suddenly the silence between them was full of tension and they stared at one another. François pressed one of her hands to his lips and kissed it.

Annie jumped up from the bunk, banging her head in her haste. 'I must tell the surgeon,' she stuttered, looking down at the floor and blushing. François rose too but he wouldn't leave go of her hand and he drew her towards him. They stood very close together in the cramped cabin and Annie could feel his breath on her face and the warmth of his body.

At last, François released her and they stood looking at one another. Then François smiled and held her close again. 'I will protect you, Annie. I will look after you.'

'Thank you for saying that, François,' she said quietly. Then, remembering her grim errand, she said,

'Will you come with me to see the surgeon and the captain?'

The surgeon was in his dispensary. He looked up when they approached and frowned. 'Yes?'

'It's my father,' said Annie, biting back the tears that threatened to overwhelm her.

'Your father is worse?' The remark was said without surprise.

'My father is dead,' said Annie.

The surgeon looked at her properly then. He put down the book he was consulting. 'I am very sorry to hear that, mistress. He was a good man.'

It was the first time since Annie had met the surgeon that she had seen him show any compassion.

'And,' Annie continued, 'my mother is delivered of a boy.'

The surgeon looked startled. 'She has had the child? That is indeed good news. Are they both well? Who attended her?'

'Yes, they are well. And we attended her. Our servant, May, and I. But May delivered the baby.'

The surgeon was still looking at her, clearly taking in her dishevelled state. She smoothed back her hair and put up the other hand to hide the torn bodice. 'I snared my dress on a nail in my hurry to come down to the orlop deck,' she said, blushing at the lie and at the memory of Michel Swarts's hand on her body.

François came to her rescue. 'I'll take her back to her cabin,' he said. 'And I'll go and inform the captain.'

'I shall be there directly,' said the surgeon. 'I shall need to collect a few things from here.'

As Annie and François passed through the gun deck, Annie peered nervously into the darkness surrounding the mainmast, but there was no sign of Michel. Nor further in, where groups of sailors were huddled round the cannons or resting in their hammocks. François was following her gaze.

'By Christ, Annie, if I find out who did this to you I won't answer for the consequences.'

'It's no good, François, I'll not reveal his name.'

When they reached her cabin, François drew her to him again.

'François, careful! Someone will see us.'

'Let them,' he said. And he kissed her gently on the lips. She was trembling when, at last, they drew apart, but this time it was not from fear.

'I'll go and inform the captain,' said François, his voice husky.

When Annie entered the cabin, May was beside Susan, who was sleeping, the baby at her breast, also asleep. It made a pretty picture.

'She's exhausted,' said May. 'I fetched her a wine caudle and as soon as she had drunk that, she slept.'

'And the little fellow too,' said Annie, smiling at

the abandonment of the baby's posture.

'Aye,' said May, and then she looked at Annie properly. 'You're very flushed, Mistress Annie. And heavens, what has happened to your dress?'

'I snagged it on a nail,' said Annie quickly.

'Snagged it on a nail?' repeated May. Annie knew that May didn't believe her and the silence lay heavy between them.

'I'd better mend it then,' said May at last.

A little later, the surgeon arrived. He looked briefly at Susan and the baby and then he confirmed that Andries was dead. He had brought two seamen with him and between them they took the body away. Annie and May watched silently.

'Should we not wake your mother?' asked May.

But Annie shook her head. Susan was still sleeping heavily, despite the commotion in the cabin. 'No, May, she needs her rest, and it would only distress her to see Father carted away like some carcass of meat.'

It was another hour before she woke. By this time, May had mended Annie's dress and between them they had tidied up her father's bunk.

'Mother?' said Annie softly, seeing her mother stir.

Susan woke from her drugged sleep. She smiled lazily at the sleeping baby lying in the crook of her arm and then, as the memory of the past hours came flooding back, she glanced across at the empty bunk.

'They've taken him!' she whispered.

'We thought it best,' said Annie. 'There was nothing more we could do for him and the surgeon will make sure he is prepared . . .'

'Prepared?'

Annie swallowed. 'Prepared for burial,' she said, choking on the word.

Susan nodded and turned away to hide her tears. She lifted the sleeping baby to her and held him tight.

Chapter Nine

It had been some time since the last sea burial, the crew being better fed on this leg of the journey and their health much improved since they had left the tropics.

The ceremony was longer and more elaborate than that of the crewmen. Andries was buried in a coffin, not simply stitched into sailcloth, and the ship's drummer called the crowd to attention. Annie was supporting her mother, who was still very weak from the birth, and May stood on her other side, holding the baby. They watched in silence as the preacher said the words they had heard so often but, when the coffin was slipped over the edge, Susan let out a loud groan and buried her head in Annie's shoulder. The shouts from the topmen continued throughout the short service and, not for the first time, Annie wondered at their callousness.

'Could they not keep their voices down, at least?' she muttered. But she knew the answer. Nothing, not even the burial of a passenger, was allowed to interfere with the onward progress of the ship.

The ceremony over, the officers and crew dispersed to their duties. Susan spoke quietly to Annie. 'I shall go back to the cabin now.'

'Mother?' Annie's heart was so full she couldn't form the words, yet there was so much she wanted to say to her. She cleared her throat.

'Shall I take the baby for a while?'

Susan nodded. May handed over baby Andries and Annie held the sleeping baby close to her chest, his tiny body comforting her.

'I'll go below with your mother,' said May and Annie watched as May and Susan made their slow way back towards the cabin, then she walked over to the ship's rail and stared down at the water. There was no sign of her father's coffin. She had been told it was weighted down with gunshot and she was glad that it had sunk fast and they had been spared the sight of it bobbing about below them.

How they would miss him! His larger than life presence, his charm and his optimism. Her cheeks were wet with tears as she remembered his enthusiasm for the voyage, his certainty that this time all would come right. *But it didn't come right, did it, Father? And what are we to do now?*

She kissed the baby's downy head and held him close. 'What's to become of us, little Andries?' she said.

It was a question that vexed all three of them. They went first to speak to the captain but, although he was sympathetic, he told them that their future was not in his hands but in those of the VOC, since Andries had been a Company employee. So next they approached the undermerchant, Jan Liebent, who was employed by the VOC, but he was evasive.

'Best to wait until we reach Java,' he said, stroking his beard. 'Once we are there you can speak with those in authority.'

'And what do you think will happen?' said Susan, exasperated by his refusal to commit himself. 'Shall we be sent back to Zeeland?'

Jan Liebent had shrugged. 'Who knows? Is that what you wish?'

Susan's voice was on the edge of hysteria. 'The last thing I wish is to spend another year of my life incarcerated in another accursed ship.'

Annie put a hand on her mother's arm. 'Hush, Mother. There may be some sort of employment for us in Java.'

'Employment?' Susan looked at her in astonishment. 'What do you mean, employment?'

Annie swallowed. 'Without Father's income, how else shall we survive?'

Susan turned to the undermerchant. 'The Company will help us with money, surely?'

Jan Liebent shrugged again. 'There may be some compensation due to you,' he said, not meeting her eyes.

And with that they had to be content. From then on, Susan fretted night and day about their future and she never let the subject rest. Annie and May were just as worried but they were sick of talking about it. One day, Annie's patience snapped.

'We can do nothing until we reach Java, Mother,' she said harshly. 'And if need be, you and I can sew well enough and May's a good servant; if we cannot afford to keep her, then I am sure others would be happy to employ her.'

May looked up in alarm, but kept her thoughts to herself. Annie sighed and picked up baby Andries, who had sensed the tension around him and was bawling. 'I'll take him out for some air,' she said shortly, and she strapped him to her chest, so that her hands were free, and climbed out on to the deck.

She paced restlessly up and down, her thoughts turning angrily to her father. *Why did you always let us down, Father? All your life you've let us down and now, in death, you've done nothing to provide for us.*

But even as she cursed him, she wept for the love of him. Feckless he may have been, but he was an adventurer, a loving adventurer who always thought that everything would come right in the end, even though he was proved wrong time and again, as his plans fell apart. Annie smiled. She couldn't be angry with him for long. His pleasant nature, his love and his incurable optimism outweighed his hopelessness with money. She looked down at her little brother and smiled. 'He would have loved you, Andries. Grow strong for him.'

Then she sniffed and wiped her eyes. She would have to be strong, too. More and more, Susan was looking to her for decisions, seemingly too grief stricken and worried to be able to think straight herself.

Annie took a deep breath and looked around for François; he was nowhere to be seen, but she spotted Lucas on the quarterdeck and she climbed up to join him. He had his back to her and he didn't see her approach so she had a moment to look at him unobserved. She could swear he'd grown taller since they left the Cape. When at last he noticed her, he straightened up from what he was doing and smiled, much less awkward, now, in her presence. He came over to her and peered at Andries, who stared up at him, hiccoughed and stopped crying.

'He's a fine lad,' said Lucas.

'He is. And my father would have been proud of him.'

Lucas dropped his gaze. 'I'm sorry . . .' he stuttered.

'Yes,' said Annie quietly. 'We all miss him.' Then she abruptly changed the subject. 'You are looking well, Lucas. Are they feeding you better now?'

'Aye, Mistress Annie. The rations are more and the climate is better, too.'

Annie nodded. 'It's some weeks since we had a lesson, Lucas. I'll bring some writing materials up here next time.'

Lucas looked at his feet and Annie was about to say something else when her attention was caught by an enormous bird, hovering on the wind close by to the ship.

'Look, Lucas! I have never seen so vast a bird. Do you know what it is?' Lucas shook his head and together they watched it. It had a powerful beak, the feathers on its back were dark but its underside was white and its wingspan more than the height of a man. Others were watching, too, and a small group of seamen paused briefly, in their work to observe it, whispering among themselves and pointing.

Annie turned to them. 'What is it?' she asked.

One of them spoke up. 'It's an albatross, mistress – the mariner's friend.' Then, as he turned away, he muttered, 'Pray God it will bring us good fortune.'

'Aye,' said another. 'We shall need it.'

Annie frowned; the seamen's words had made her uneasy. Surely now, when they were making good headway and the crew were better fed, their fortunes had improved, had they not, even if the fortunes of her own family were so uncertain?

The group of men moved off and Andries began to fret and wriggle in Annie's arms.

'I'd better go below now, Lucas. The little one is hungry and needs his mother.'

A few weeks later, the *Zuytdorp* abruptly changed course. All hands were on deck and there was much shouting and cursing as the great ship was swung round to head north. It was not long after this that Annie sensed the change in the weather. While it was not cold – in the way that it was cold in her native Zeeland in winter – and the skies were often cloudless and blue, the atmosphere was certainly fresher.

One day, François and Annie stood together by the ship's rail. Annie had little Andries strapped to her chest and he was grizzling and fractious; François smiled down at him.

'The last lap, little man. Soon we shall be at our journey's end.'

'Pray God there will be no more mishaps,' said Annie.

François didn't answer, and she turned to him, frowning.

'Is something wrong?'

'No.'

'Come now. I know you too well. Something's troubling you.'

He shook his head but she persisted. 'I shall go on asking until you tell me,' she said, smiling.

He shrugged. 'Just old seamen's talk.'

'And of what do they talk?'

'Oh, some who have been this way before say that the captain should not have taken this course from the Cape, that it is too late in the season and that we may encounter winter storms off the coast of the Great Southland.'

Annie nodded. 'I remember there was discontent on board when he set the course from the Cape. Do *you* think that the captain has made the right decision, François?'

He smiled down at her. 'As you have often pointed out to me, Annie, I have never made this voyage before – but my instinct is to trust the captain's judgement rather than the gossip of the crew.'

Annie put up a hand to stroke his face and he held it fast.

'Will you be a captain one day, François?'

'Aye. God willing.' Then he lowered his voice.

'And a better one than Wysvliet.'

'Captain François Carel de Bruijn,' said Annie slowly. 'It sounds well.'

François laughed. 'That day is a long way off, Annie. First I have to take my lieutenant's exams and then I shall have to go to sea many more times before I can take command of a ship.'

Gently, Annie took her hand away from his face. She looked down at the baby, who was quiet at last. 'We shall wait for you,' she said quietly.

François came closer to her. 'Will you really wait for me, Annie?'

She looked up at him again and saw the uncertainty in his eyes. 'Of course I will,' she said steadily.

They stood close together for a few moments, looking out to sea. In the far distance they could see land.

'What is out there, François, in the Unknown Land?'

'Emptiness,' he said. 'As far as anyone knows the land is arid and barren.' He stretched his arms above his head and continued, 'Though, years ago, there were two mutineers set ashore along this coast.'

Annie looked up sharply. 'Mutineers? From a Company ship?'

'Aye, a ship called the *Batavia*. She ran aground on a reef in these parts some eighty years ago and, when the captain and commander and officers set sail for Java in the longboat, the undermerchant led a terrible mutiny and massacre. When the commander returned with a rescue ship, those who had remained loyal were rewarded but most of the mutineers were hanged – except for the two young men who he deliberately marooned.'

Annie shivered. 'And does anyone know what became of them?'

'No. They were never heard of again. They were given supplies and told to make contact with native tribes.'

'What a fate! Does anyone know if there *are* native tribes?'

'Oh, there are plenty of rumours. The seamen who have travelled this route swear they have seen smoke from distant fires. And there was some talk of the ruins of an ancient city.'

'An ancient city? How can that be?'

François laughed. 'I have no idea, Annie. It's probably all nonsense. And, God willing, we shall never have to set foot on the shore of the Unknown Land – so we are never likely to find out.'

It was only a few days later, when this conversation was still fresh in her mind, that Captain Wysvliet called her over to him. She had just climbed up from her cabin on to the poop deck so she could hardly avoid his summons. Since her father's death, Captain

Wysvliet had shown her more kindness than before, but Annie was still wary of him. She hesitated and he called again.

'Come over here, Annie. This is a sight I never thought to see.' There was excitement in his voice as he handed her his eyeglass.

'There. Look straight ahead and inland. What do you see?'

Frowning, Annie clamped the glass to her eye and stared. At first, everything was out of focus and all she could see was the water. But then, as she looked more carefully and, under the captain's instructions, raised the eyeglass and trained it on what was beyond the sand dunes and further inland, she gasped. There were hundreds and hundreds of stone forms, thrusting up from the ground, etched against the sky.

'It is the ancient city, is it not? François told me about it.'

Captain Wysvliet smiled and took the glass from her, putting it to his eye again.

'I doubt it is an ancient city, Annie, but whatever it is, it cannot easily be explained. It is a strange and wondrous sight, is it not?'

Annie nodded.

'I've heard about this from other mariners,' continued the captain, 'but I never thought to see it for myself.'

Annie lowered the eyeglass slowly. 'What a strange country,' she murmured.

'Indeed it is,' agreed Wysvliet. 'A great barren empty land.'

'Have ships stopped along its shore?' asked Annie.

Wysvliet shrugged. 'A few. At first the Company thought to explore its potential for trading goods, but there is nothing there.'

'Nothing?'

'As far as we can tell. And if there are native tribes, they keep themselves well hidden and are savages with no learning or goods to trade.'

'I wonder what happened to those two mutineers?'

Wysvliet looked down at her. 'You've heard of those *Batavia* fellows, have you?'

She nodded. 'François told me.'

Wysvliet cleared his throat and snapped his eyeglass shut. 'They were probably eaten by savages or died of starvation,' he said.

Annie didn't answer and looked out towards the coastline again. What a fate; to be marooned on such a hostile shore. For the rest of the day her thoughts kept returning to the two young men. Were they friends? Did they hate each other? Did they become part of a local tribe or were they killed by them? She kept imagining them, facing the emptiness and strangeness, and she was filled by a sense of foreboding she could not shake off.

By the next day, the blue sky had turned grey and the wind had freshened. François was much occupied in carrying out orders to secure everything in the ship against the worsening weather, but he snatched a few moments to be with Annie. The ship was beginning to pitch and roll in the swell, but so far it was no worse than the movement they'd experienced in the cold North Sea at the beginning of their journey. Annie stared at the coast, where there was a line of great red sandstone cliffs so different from the grey cliffs they had seen before and, in particular, a huge jutting headland. She pointed to it and asked François about it but her voice was snatched away by the wind. She shouted her question again and this time he heard.

'They call that the Red High,' he yelled. 'It's a landmark to the seamen.' Then he turned and looked anxiously in the opposite direction. Annie turned too, and followed his gaze, seeing great black clouds rolling in towards them. The wind was strengthening all the time and the ship was lurching beneath their feet. François took her by the shoulders.

'Go back to your cabin, Annie. There's a storm coming.'

She nodded. 'Be careful,' she mouthed at him as she staggered back over the deck towards the hatchway that led down to the cabin. A sudden gust of wind caught her and she banged her shoulder against unyielding wood, letting out a cry of pain, but her cry was swallowed up by the increasing noise of the storm. She was flung from side to side once she was below and only opened the cabin door with difficulty. Inside, her mother and May were wide eyed with fright. May had secured everything she could but even so, there were loose items hurtling about in the tiny space and the baby was screaming and would not be comforted.

'Lord, Mistress Annie,' gasped May. 'This is worse than those storms in the North Sea, is it not?'

'I'm sure we shall weather it, May, as we weathered the others,' said Annie, trying to sound reassuring. But all the time, in the back of her mind, she was thinking of the warnings about winter storms along this coast and of François's worried face.

They all lay in their bunks, hanging on to the sides, waiting for the storm to subside, but it continued to gain strength. There was one hideous lurch which threw them all out on to the floor of the cabin. Annie was the first to recover and she snatched baby Andries from where he had fallen.

'Is he all right?' yelled Susan.

'Yes. I think so, Mother,' she said as she tried to comfort the screaming child. 'Just frightened.' She stayed on the floor and held the baby to her chest and then reached for the strips of linen that she used to tie him to her, this time strapping him in much more securely than she had ever done before. Andries was bawling with fright and Annie tried in vain to comfort him, kissing his head and wrapping her arms around him.

The three women stayed where they had fallen, not daring to climb back into their bunks. May and Susan were both whimpering with terror.

'Oh Lord, what will become of us?' muttered Susan. But no one heard her. The noise of the storm and the creaking of the ship's timbers drowned her out. Then, suddenly, there was another violent crash as the ship caught a wave head on and the cabin lurched violently to one side.

'Help! God have mercy on us,' screamed May. 'We are going to die, mistress.'

It was unrelenting now. There was no let-up in the lurching and plunging and, even though they were below, they could still hear the screaming of the wind and the sound of the protesting timbers. Annie was fully employed trying to keep Andries from harm but her own body was being battered and bruised as she was flung from side to side. Then there was an even more violent lurch and Annie saw some water coming in from under the door. May had noticed it, too.

'Look!' she screamed. 'The ship's taking on water. We shall all be drowned, like rats in a barrel.'

Annie tried to think through her terror as she watched the water seeping in over the floor. It was coming in faster and faster. She crawled towards the door.

'What are you doing, Annie?' screamed her mother. But Annie took no notice.

'For God's sake, girl, don't open the door.'

Annie closed her ears to her mother's pleas and May's screams. At last she reached the cabin door and pulled it open. A flood of water poured in.

'We must go up on deck,' she yelled. 'If we stay here we shall drown.'

'Annie!' screamed Susan, now sitting in the swirling water, which came up to her waist. Annie looked back and held out her arm. 'Hold on to me,' she said.

But Susan was frozen with fear and Annie couldn't drag her up. 'May,' she shouted. 'Make her come. Hurry.'

'Don't go on deck, Mistress Annie. Please stay here.'

Annie turned back and as she did so, another wave of water hit her.

'We must get out of here,' she yelled as she was thrust forward. 'Come ON!'

Somehow, she slithered and crashed her way to the hatchway but as she pushed from below to open it, she realized that it had been battened down from the deck side. Frantically, she pummelled on the wood, clawing at it, shrieking, but there was no way she could get out and no one on deck would hear her cries among the turmoil and noise. Drenched and terrified, she huddled at the bottom of the steps beneath the hatch.

'François,' she yelled. But there was no answering cry. Then there was another juddering roll of the ship and if she'd not had a firm grip on the steps she would have been hurled backwards on to the wooden planks. She looked over her shoulder, back towards the cabin. 'Mother!' she yelled. But there was no sign of her mother or of May.

Andries had stopped his full blooded yelling and was whimpering and staring up at her with huge eyes. She didn't dare lose her hold on the stairs to comfort him but she bent down quickly to kiss his cheek. 'Oh God, please let him live,' she prayed silently.

She didn't hear it at first, among the other noises, but gradually she became aware that someone was scraping back the bolts that held the hatch. She gasped and put one hand into the widening gap, still clinging to the stair with the other. Someone gripped her hand and heaved and, as the hatch was pulled aside, she saw François's anxious face staring down at her. Sobbing with relief, she struggled out but she couldn't stand upright on deck and immediately fell to her knees.

'François!'

He was dishevelled and bruised, his hair matted

to his head. 'Annie,' he said, shouting above the wind. 'There's no time; quick – climb as far as you can up the rigging and hold on there for your life.'

'What?'

'Do as I say.'

'But my mother – and May.'

'I'll see to them. Now quickly. There's no time to lose.' Then he was gone, down the hatchway.

Slithering, crawling, holding on to anything that gave her solid purchase, Annie headed for the rigging, all the time trying to protect the wriggling baby at her chest. There was another huge lurch and she lost her grip and was propelled across the deck, just saved from going overboard by the ship's rail that was, at that moment, pointing skywards; from there it was not far to some rigging. She flung herself at it and started to climb, her cuts and bruises ignored and her terror giving her strength she didn't know she had. She was not alone. There were passengers and sailors beside her, all jostling for space, screaming and shouting. Momentarily she was aware of a burning pain in her skinned hands. She saw chaos all around her – men running hither and thither, sliding all over the decks, which were tilted at a wild angle, shouting and swearing – and then she heard a chilling cry from the steersman. 'We can't turn her. The wind's too strong. We're going to run aground.'

Now it was each man for himself, everyone grabbing on to something to keep them from being thrown overboard. More men started to climb the rigging and Annie was jostled and crushed but she clung on like a limpet, her eyes straining to see ahead through the darkness of the sky and the spray which drenched her.

Then there was a flash of lightning and suddenly the high coastal cliffs towering up in front of them could be seen clearly and, beneath them, lying like some sinister grey sacrificial altar, a great flat table of rock, jutting out into the water.

'God help us, Andries,' she whispered and she braced herself for the impact which she knew would come any moment.

But nothing could have prepared her for the force of that great ship as it met the shelf of rock and reared up, its prow pointing to the sky, flinging Annie and the baby – and so many others – out into the water.

Chapter Ten

The only thought that pierced through the terror as she was propelled into the air was that the baby at her chest would die. All the breath was driven from her body as she tumbled towards the water and then hit it with an impact that winded her again. There wasn't time to scream before they were both under the swirling, boiling waves. Then as the sea drew back to crash again on to the shore, she bobbed up like a cork for a moment and managed to take a spluttering breath before she was under again, her body first spun around and then flung forward further towards the shore.

Again, she came up for breath, and this time she felt the hard shelf of rock beneath her feet for a moment, until she was sucked under once more. Then, the next time, she was facing the shore when her head broke through the water and, as soon as her feet touched the rock, she pushed forward with all her strength.

It was not far to the shore. If only she could stay upright through the swirling water and reach it before the next wave pounded down on her from behind.

But she was too late. Again, a wave engulfed her and she and the baby were tossed about like so much else – debris from the ship, barrels, planks, chests and already some poor, drowned folk. Annie couldn't swim and she knew that her only chance was to stay on her feet, but she was losing her strength. She was exhausted and her nose and mouth were full of seawater. As the next wave receded, it seemed that she was further back than before and her sobs mingled with the roar of the storm. She didn't dare look at the baby; he was still fastened to her but he was limp and a dead weight and she was sure he could not have survived the pummelling.

When she could next feel the rock beneath her, she scraped her leg on a vertical outcrop. Instinctively, she recoiled from it, but then her numbed brain reacted. If she could just hold on to it and save herself from being sucked backwards again, maybe she could make it to the shore the next time. The water was shallow here and she knelt down in it and clung on to the sharp rock with both hands, making sure that Andries's head was clear of the water. Just as the next wave was about to hit them from behind, the baby suddenly spluttered and Annie's heart leapt at the tiny triumph.

Hold on, Andries!

When the wave hit them they went under again, but this time Annie had hold of the rock and she managed to resist the water's pull. Then, as it dragged back and the water was once again shallow, she staggered to her feet and splashed forward, running, tripping, scraping her feet and shins, but going forward, desperate to beat the water. She had nearly reached the shore when she tripped and fell forward and she could hear the water coming in again behind her. But this time she could see more jagged rocks on the shoreline and she grabbed one and pulled herself forward, then upright, just in time to jump free and on to the shore.

She kept going forward, blood streaming from her cut hands and feet, and didn't stop until she could go no further. In front of her was a great rugged cliff like an enormous earthy wall and, at its foot, huge boulders and a little sand. Annie sat down against the base of the cliff, whimpering, and with numb fingers tried to unstrap Andries. He was too quiet, and she feared the worst. When at last she had loosed him, she put him over her knees and gently massaged his back. At first there was no movement, but then suddenly his whole body was consumed by a spasm of coughing. She held him in her arms then, as he vomited up seawater, his little face puckered with fury; and he screamed lustily as she rocked him, trying to comfort him.

'Thank God you are alive,' she whispered, holding him as close as she could, to give him some warmth from her own body, though she herself was shivering from the wet and cold and terror of it.

It was some time before she could bring herself to focus on the scene in front of her. What she saw was like some depiction of hell; there were bodies in the water, being thrown about just as she had been, many of them apparently lifeless, and so many goods from the hold which had burst free and were being tossed about in the cauldron of wild white water, and beyond them the great *Zuytdorp*, wedged against the rock platform, being pounded by the relentless waves.

She dragged her gaze back to the shore. There was little movement around her. Any who had managed to reach safety were, like her, exhausted by their ordeal and they were lying prone on the ground, retching up seawater or sitting propped up against the base of the cliff. The minutes passed and the only sound was that of the waves and the storm and the wind – and occasionally a desperate cry from some poor soul still in the water. But no one could help. The water was wild and to go in again to try and save another was to risk almost certain death.

Then, along the shore from her, Annie saw a man get to his feet and walk uncertainly from survivor to survivor.

The uppersteersman, Melchior Haijensz.

'Thank God, Andries,' said Annie. 'At least there is someone who can take charge.'

She looked around her, staring at each person as they crawled around on the sand and among the rocks, or stood upright, some limping from injuries, some holding their heads and rocking to and fro, moaning.

François has surely rescued Mother and May, she thought, but there was no sign of them and, as the day wore on and a few more survivors made it ashore, still they did not come.

'Oh God, baby, what shall we do if my mother is lost?' she muttered. 'You cannot survive without her milk.'

And May? And François?

She closed her eyes and prayed for their safety. Prayed as she had never done before.

'Dear God,' she whispered. 'If I have ever done aught to please thee, help me now and save those I love.'

But the only answer was the screaming wind and the pounding of the surf as it hit the shore.

Gradually, Melchior started to assemble the surviving seamen and soldiers and ordered them to fetch any wood from the ship which had been flung ashore and drag it further up the beach. And she saw two men scrambling up the cliff and then, later, coming back to report. Then more were sent up and they returned with armfuls of brushwood and disappeared with it further along the shore.

Annie sat motionless, her gaze hardly leaving the stricken ship and the seething water, as more bodies were washed ashore and dragged away out of sight, under Melchior's instructions.

Will someone tell me if François or Mother or May are among them?

The baby soiled himself but Annie had not the strength to do anything about it. In any case, what could she do? There was no clean linen or dry clothes. For a while she continued to cling to him fiercely, shivering from shock and cold, but then her grip loosened, her head dropped on to her chest and she and the baby both drifted off into an uneasy and exhausted sleep.

She was woken by someone shaking her arm.

'Get up, mistress.'

She came back to consciousness gradually, only slowly taking in the horror before her.

A man was standing in front of her, his face gashed, and the hand that shook her arm was bruised and swollen. Annie didn't know his name; he was one of the new recruits taken on at the Cape.

'The uppersteersman has sent me to fetch you, mistress.' He put his arm under her elbow and made to raise her.

Annie shook herself awake. 'I can manage,' she said, getting up awkwardly, the weight of the baby making her clumsy.

The man pointed to the south. 'There's a bit of a beach round the corner, with some rocks for shelter. And we've made a merry fire; one of the men saved a tinderbox.'

A merry fire? thought Annie. *As if anything can be merry now.* But she shuffled along beside him as he led her round the point, her stiff limbs reluctant to obey her.

The man was right. There was a broader patch of beach here and there was, indeed, a fire, though it could hardly be called merry, for the brushwood with which it had been started soon turned to ash and the timbers salvaged from the water were still damp and hissing.

She looked round at the group of survivors and she could only see a few familiar faces. Jan Liebent, the undermerchant, was the only Company man among them and she supposed that he would be in charge now, for there was no sign of the captain or of the surgeon or of any of the other officers.

There were two midshipmen among the party, but

François was not one of them.

Jan Liebent, the undermerchant, saw her arrive and came up to her. 'God be praised you have survived, Annie.' He looked at the baby. 'And the little one, too.'

She shook her head sadly. 'He needs his mother's milk,' she said.

They said nothing then. What was there to say? At last, Jan broke the silence. 'We've had a count of the survivors and there are seventy-four so far, but many are badly injured.'

'And the surgeon?' asked Annie. 'Is he here?'

Jan shook his head. 'No. Nor his assistant.'

Again there was silence. But there was an unspoken question between them and finally Annie gave voice to it. 'Then who will tend the wounded?' she asked, knowing the answer well enough.

Jan cleared his throat. 'I know that Jacob thought highly of your nursing skills. Perhaps . . .?'

He put his hand on her shoulder. 'It will be dark soon and there's nothing much you can do before daylight, but then . . .'

She sighed. 'I'll do my best.'

'Thank you. '

'Meanwhile,' continued Jan, 'some sailcloth has been washed ashore from the hold and the men have dried it as best they can. It will afford a little shelter, at least.'

'Thank you,' she said and she and Andries moved off towards the fire. The light was beginning to fade now and the faces of the people on the beach were indistinct, but still she kept looking for her mother and May – and François.

Suddenly someone jumped up from the circle of folk huddled nearest the fire and came running towards her.

'Mistress Annie! They said you were alive but I didn't believe them. I thought you were lost, too!'

'Lucas!'

Seeing the boy standing there in front of her, Annie couldn't hold back the tears any longer and she dropped to her knees and sobbed.

Lucas stood beside her awkwardly. 'Please don't cry, mistress,' he said at last.

She smiled through her tears. 'Aye, Lucas, I should not cry. We're alive, at least. And I am glad of it, of course I am.'

Not knowing what else to say, Lucas blurted out, 'And you can go on teaching me my letters.'

Annie laughed. 'Oh, Lucas! We are half drowned, we have no idea whether we shall survive, but you talk of learning your letters!'

Lucas looked down at his feet. 'I thought to cheer you,' he muttered.

'And you did, Lucas. You did.'

Lucas showed her where the pile of sailcloth lay, under the shelter of some rocks. There were already other survivors huddled under it, some moaning, some whispering among themselves.

'Stay here with me, Lucas,' said Annie.

'But . . .'

'For goodness' sake, boy. This is no time for keeping to conventions,' she snapped. 'Now help me unstrap the baby and clean him.'

Given a job to do, Lucas sprang into action. He found the bottom of a broken barrel and filled it with seawater from one of the rock pools and then, between them, they stripped Andries and cleaned him as best they could before wrapping him up in sailcloth. By now the baby was whimpering with hunger but there was nothing Annie could do to help him. Annie handed him to Lucas.

'Hold him for a while, Lucas. I must get out of these sodden clothes or I shall die of the ague.' Then she added, under her breath, 'If I don't die first of starvation or infection.'

Awkwardly, Lucas took the baby and, in the lee of one of the rocks, Annie stripped down to her shift. She spread the rest of her clothes on the surface of the rock and weighted them down with loose stones. The wind had dropped now and the rain had stopped; with luck, tomorrow would bring the sun again to dry them out.

She went back to Lucas and the baby and the three of them huddled together for warmth under the sailcloth.

All around them they heard murmurs from the others. The talk was mostly of food.

'There are oysters among the rocks here,' said one of the seamen. 'We can gather those in the morning.'

Then one of the party, who had climbed up on to the cliff top, spoke. 'Aye, and we saw some strange, hopping creatures on the land above the cliffs. If any muskets are saved we could shoot these for food.'

'Hopping creatures?' asked another.

'Aye. With little pointed faces and great back legs and tiny forepaws.'

'Huh,' his companion laughed harshly. 'That bang on the head has addled your brain!'

Before night fell, Melchior, the uppersteersman, came round to each group of survivors in turn, reaching Annie and Lucas last. He crouched down beside them and offered Annie his water bottle. 'We have a little fresh water, Annie; a couple of barrels came ashore intact.' Annie took the water bottle and put it gratefully to her parched lips. Then she dribbled a little into Andries's mouth, but the baby spluttered and spat. 'Take it, you silly boy,' she urged him, and at last she managed to get him to swallow a few tiny draughts.

Melchior watched them. 'Jan Liebent tells me you have offered to tend the sick, Annie. There will be much work for you to do in the morning. Are you sure you are strong enough?'

Annie's cuts and bruises were throbbing and, although the air here was hardly like the cold winters she had known in Zeeland, she was still shivering from being soaked through and her long hair hung damply down her back. But she replied bravely through chattering teeth:

'If Lucas will help me, and maybe one or two of the seamen as well, under my instruction, we shall manage, I'm sure.' She handed the water bottle to Lucas.

He took a long swig. 'I have no skill in –' he began, but Annie put a hand on his arm to still him.

'I'll teach you, Lucas.' Then she looked down at Andries, bundled up in sailcloth. She wiped the drops of water from his mouth.

'Without his mother's milk he cannot live,' she said quietly.

Melchior straightened up and pressed his hand briefly on her shoulder. 'I'll leave the water with you and then in the morning we shall see what can be done,' he said.

But Annie knew that there was nothing they could do. Fresh water might keep him alive for a while, but he was too young to take any other food. She lay on her back with Andries in her arms and looked up at the inky sky. It was clear now, and the stars were appearing; such a different night sky from that in her native Zeeland. She was hungry and cold; but so was everyone else. Gradually the talking around her stopped and Lucas's breathing deepened. The only noises were the groans of wounded men and the pounding of the waves.

'Please God,' she prayed, 'let François be alive. And Mother, and my lovely May.'

Chapter Eleven

Annie was woken early by the baby's cries; weak now, no longer the lusty yells that had sometimes filled the cabin on board ship. She turned towards him and cradled him, then gave him more water from the bottle that Melchior had left with them, though she knew this wouldn't satisfy him. She lay there for a while, listening to the sounds around her – of men waking, of groaning, and of the waves. The early morning sky was bright and clear and there was only a light breeze coming off the sea. A complete contrast to the black skies, vivid lightning and screaming winds of yesterday. For a moment she felt cheered, but then the weight of sadness returned; how could she bear the loss of her family and of François? She looked at Lucas, still asleep beside her, then, leaving Andries on the ground, she struggled to her feet.

She was not the first to wake. She looked around the beach and saw that Jan Liebent and Melchior had already assembled most of the able bodied seamen and soldiers around them and were giving them instructions. Annie retrieved her clothes from the rock; they were still damp and she shivered as she put them on. Then, picking up the whimpering baby, she went over to the group.

Both Melchior and Jan looked strained and pale. Melchior acknowledged her with a curt nod but Jan ignored her and continued to speak to the men.

'Our first priority is to gather food,' he was saying. 'You there, gather as many oysters as you can and see if there is any way we can trap fish; and you two,' he said, pointing at a couple of bedraggled soldiers, 'go and see if any muskets have been washed up and if they can be made to work. Then, if they are serviceable, climb up to the cliff top and see if you can shoot some animals for food.'

He and Melchior kept giving further instructions. Men were to salvage anything they could reach without endangering themselves and to haul everything up beyond the waterline. They were to look out especially for more intact barrels of water. Others were to fetch brushwood from the cliff top and any timber that had washed ashore and then to relight and tend the fire. Another group was charged with dragging any corpses out of the water or from the shoreline, and trying to identify them. Then Jan addressed the two midshipmen.

'And you two are to supervise the groups,' he said.

When the men had dispersed, Jan turned to Melchior. 'Annie will be able to do little for the wounded without linen and medicine –' he began.

Annie interrupted him. 'If you let me instruct a couple of men,' she said, 'we can make splints from driftwood and bind them with sailcloth, at least. It will make those with broken limbs more comfortable.'

Jan nodded. 'Very well. I'll see who I can find.'

'And Lucas will help me,' said Annie firmly.

'Lucas?'

'The ship's boy.'

Jan turned to Melchior. 'The ship's boy? Can that scrawny lad do anything more useful than cleaning out animals?'

Annie flared up with anger. 'Indeed he can,' she retorted then, more quietly, she said, 'If you send two helpers to me, we can start work as soon as I have inspected the bodies of the dead.'

'Why waste time on them –?' began Jan.

But Melchior stopped him. 'She'll want to see if her family are among them,' he said quietly.

Jan shrugged. He was only concerned with the living.

Steeling herself, Annie walked back round the point to the place where she had been flung ashore. First she went up to the midshipman who was supervising the dragging ashore of the dead bodies. Already there was a sizeable heap by the bottom of the cliff. The midshipman knew Annie.

'Don't come near here,' he said kindly. 'It is no sight for a young girl.'

'I have seen bodies before,' said Annie firmly. 'You know that.'

'Aye,' he replied quietly, 'but not ones so battered as these.'

'I just want to know if my mother is among them. Or our servant May, or . . .' and she hesitated, 'or François Carel de Bruijn.'

The young midshipman shook his head. 'There are no women here. And nor is François among the dead.'

A tiny flicker of hope sprang up in Annie's heart but it was soon dashed by the midshipman's next remark.

'It doesn't mean much, though,' he said. 'Many of the dead would have been trapped below decks.' He looked down dispassionately at the heap in front of him. 'And any crew on the gun deck would have been crushed by loose cannon if they weren't drowned.'

She said nothing but walked away. The *Zuytdorp* had swivelled round and was now broadside on to the shore and only the mast, sails and rigging were still above the water, leaning at a drunken angle. She could see now where the ship had hit the great table of flat rock that ran into the shore. The waves were still big, but less wild than yesterday, and they were crashing against it before running on. There were men everywhere, among the great boulders on the shore and wading in the shallow waters at the sea's edge, heaving out barrels and other loose items, swearing and shouting, being constantly drenched with spray while they worked. The poor ship had spilled out her guts and there was a mass of stuff being tossed about and swirling in the water. In among the barrels and other debris, Annie could make out a glint of silver on the flat rock beneath the surface and she thought back to the time when she had crept down to the ship's hold and seen the heavy chests.

The silver would never pay for goods in the Indies now.

Suddenly she heard a piercing scream and she looked up sharply, as did all the men working. She strained her eyes to see who had made such a noise, but there was no sign of anyone in trouble. Then one of the seamen who was sorting things near the cliff ran down to the shore.

'Be careful,' he yelled. 'I saw what happened.' He pointed away to the right.

'He was sucked down. I saw it. Don't go near there.'

For a moment, the men stopped working. 'What is it? How did he go under?'

An older seaman looked over to the place where the man had disappeared. 'There must be blowholes in the rock,' he said. 'A blowhole can suck a man down in an instant.'

Annie shivered. It had all happened so quickly. What treachery there was in this sea!

As the morning wore on, Annie was kept busy instructing Lucas and the two sailors who had been assigned to her. She explained what she needed and then she set off to examine the wounded. Those that could be moved had been put in the lee of one of the largest rocks near what was now their camp, by the fire. So that she could get on with her work, she put Andries down in the shade of a rock. He was unnaturally still and quiet.

Now that it was daylight, Annie could see all the survivors clearly and she was guiltily relieved that, as far as she could tell, Michel, the German soldier who had assaulted her, was not among them. She could move freely now, without having to watch out for him. Although she would not wish anyone dead, she knew she would have been more at risk from him in this desolate place where it would be difficult to apply the normal shipboard discipline.

Slowly, she, Lucas and the two seamen inspected all the sick and wounded. All they could do was to give them some fresh water, clean their wounds with saltwater and put rudimentary splints on broken limbs. It was frustrating work, for they had no medicines and nothing with which to bind wounds except some torn linen from the men's shirts; and nothing to cover their bodies with except sailcloth. Some blankets had been washed ashore but they were sodden. Annie got the seamen to make rough drying frames from salvaged timbers and they draped the blankets over these and placed them as close to the fire as possible.

In the middle of the morning, Annie took a moment to catch her breath and to check on Andries. He was asleep now but his breathing was shallow. Gently, she picked him up but he didn't stir; he was limp in her arms.

As she was standing there, cradling the baby whose life was ebbing from him, one of the men came running round the point and went to Melchior.

'Sir, sir – there are more folk alive,' he shouted.

Melchior turned, astonished. 'More folk in the water?' he said. 'How can they have survived?'

The man shook his head. 'No. Not in the water. There are two people on the ship's rigging. They are alive but they'll have to jump soon, for the rigging is lying close to the water and the ship is going down.'

They all ran, then, round the point to the wreck site. Melchior, Lucas and Annie, with the baby. As she reached the shoreline, Annie screwed up her eyes to look, again, towards the poor stricken *Zuytdorp*. There was only one small stretch of rigging above the waterline now, and clinging to it were two people.

She shaded her eyes but she couldn't make out who they were. Then someone shouted. 'One of them's a woman,' and Annie stared harder, willing the woman to be her mother – or May. She gripped the baby tightly and kept watching the figures on the rigging. She could see the woman, now, bulky in her skirts, but she couldn't make out who she was. There was another figure close beside her – a man – and it looked as though he was urging her to loosen her grip on the rigging and jump. The water wasn't far below them, for the ship was sinking fast, but the man and woman continued to be locked in what looked like a mortal struggle – until, suddenly, the woman lost her grip and tumbled off the rigging, pitching into the sea. Immediately the man jumped after her and Annie could see him striking out towards her as soon as he was in the water.

There was something about him that was familiar, the toss of his head as he rose above the waves and struck out strongly, and Annie held her breath, willing it to be François.

Please God, let it be him.

Now they were bobbing about in the water. The waves weren't as fierce as yesterday but the short stretch of water between the ship and the shore was still treacherous, whirling and sucking at them, unwilling to deliver them up from its grasp. Annie's eyes never left them. They were together again now, the man holding the woman's head above the water, forcing her forward, but the water was pulling them over to the right and Annie suddenly remembered the old seaman's warning about the blowholes.

Lucas was beside her and she thrust the baby at him. 'Hold him, Lucas!' she yelled, then she waded into the water as far as she dared.

'FRANÇOIS!' she screamed, waving her hands frantically.

The man looked up briefly, before turning back to the task of keeping the woman afloat.

Annie's heart missed a beat. It *was* him! Then it must be her mother, too!

But they were drifting nearer and nearer to the place where the man had vanished earlier. Annie cupped her hands and yelled again: 'This way!' she screamed, gesturing for him to steer away from the blowholes. But if he heard, he didn't understand; and all she could do was to keep shouting and gesticulating as they came slowly closer, being buffeted this way and that, now being thrown forward, now sucked back. Annie covered her eyes, unable to watch any more. There was nothing she could do to help them. Even if he'd understood her warning, there was no controlling the treacherous undertow; it would take him where it willed, and her mother too.

Lucas was beside her now, the limp baby still in his arms. He said nothing but just stared out at the struggling man and woman.

When she looked again, Annie saw that François had found a vertical rock to hang on to, but he could only hold it with one hand, the other being under her mother's arms. Her mother wasn't helping him. She was inert – a dead weight.

And then, when the next set of waves pushed them closer to the shore, François was crawling forward, pulling, dragging her mother with him. Annie splashed through the shallows towards them, desperate to get to them before they were dragged back again.

'François!'

He looked up. 'Take my hand,' he gasped, and she rushed forward, but Melchior held her back. 'Get back to the shore, Annie,' he shouted. 'I am stronger. I can help him.' And with that he strode forward and took François's outstretched hand firmly in his own, but Susan was thrashing about and moaning behind François, and it took the two men all their combined strength to hold her.

'Let them help you, Mother,' screamed Annie, but Susan continued to flay her arms about, too shocked and terrified to understand. Lucas had gone out as far as he dared, still holding the baby and, suddenly, Andries let out a faint cry and it was then that something connected in Susan's brain, for she heard the cry, despite the noise of the water and the shouting all about her, and she began to help herself, no longer resisting Melchior and François. She lurched forward of her own accord and they were able to haul her out of the water just as the next set of waves came crashing in towards them.

They stood, the five of them – Melchior, François, Lucas, Susan and Annie, panting with effort, at the base of the cliff. Annie went to François and put her arms round him and they held each other tightly, standing silent, both dripping seawater.

'Thank God you're safe,' he said, breaking away from her at last.

Annie couldn't speak. She was too choked up with relief.

Melchior spat out a mouthful of seawater. 'Why did you wait so long?' he asked François. 'Why did you not jump earlier?'

François was still fighting for breath. He looked across at Susan. 'She was terrified of the water – of drowning. I couldn't get her to leave the ship,' he gasped.

'So you stayed with her?'

He nodded.

Annie put her hand up to his face. 'Thank you,' she said, finding her voice at last.

He covered her hand with his own, which was scratched and bleeding. 'But I couldn't save May, Annie.'

Annie bowed her head and he went on. 'She was on deck with us but she got swept overboard last night. I fear she will have perished.'

Annie nodded silently, not trusting herself to speak, then she glanced over at her mother and a stab of fear cramped her stomach. Susan's eyes were staring and she seemed completely unaware of where she was.

'Lucas, give my mother the baby,' said Annie.

Lucas took the baby to Susan but although she automatically held out her arms for the child and took him off Lucas, there was no recognition in her blank face, and she turned away and looked out to sea.

Annie frowned.

'Come,' said Melchior to François. 'You must all get dried out. There's a fire and a rough camp to the south.'

He led the way and the others followed him. Susan shuffled along, still speechless, with the baby held loosely in her arms and Annie at her side.

When they reached the fire and Susan saw some of the other survivors, her face became less blank, but still she didn't speak. Annie helped her off with her clothes and found one of the newly dried blankets for her, then she put Andries to Susan's breast. At first Susan tried to push him away and the limp baby, in any case, seemed to have no interest in his mother's milk.

Oh, God, thought Annie. *Suppose I can't get her to suckle him?*

But gradually, she managed to make the baby latch on to his mother's breast, though it was some time before he sucked, and then it was with little energy. But he did get a bit of nourishment, at least, before his head drooped and he slept again.

'Next time he will be hungrier,' said Annie soothingly to her mother, wishing with all her heart that May had been with them. May would have persuaded Susan to feed the baby and persuaded the baby to suckle. Annie felt inexperienced and clumsy.

Suddenly, the loss of May was more than she could bear. She sank down on her knees and covered her face with her hands. *God, May, forgive me for all the harsh words I spoke. You were our rock, and I never realized it.*

Now, in this godforsaken place, she needed May. May, who with her shrewd native instinct, understood Annie better than anyone, and who had vexed and amused her in equal measure. May, who had never wanted to come on this voyage with them, who had been so seasick and so terrified of the water. But who had been there with them, seeing them through the death of her father and the birth of her brother.

I miss you so, May.

François was given little time to recover from his ordeal; he had scarcely dried out in front of the fire and supped a little fresh water before Jan Liebent and Melchior set him to work.

'Let me see to this gash on his leg at least,' said Annie angrily. But François himself was anxious to get to work.

'Nothing's broken, Annie,' he said. 'And I'm better off than many of these others.' She put a restraining hand on his arm but he drew away from her, smiling, and went to get his orders.

'Stupid boy – he's exhausted. Any fool can see that,' she muttered to no one in particular. *If only he had been able to save May, too*, she thought, but then she tried to put aside her aching grief and told herself that she should rejoice that François was alive; he was with her and he had saved her mother. She watched him limp off, hungry for his company but proud, too, of his determination.

Under Jan and Melchior's direction, the men worked tirelessly and some sort of order was established. By great good fortune, Pieter Morreij, the ship's chief carpenter, had survived and was not badly hurt. He and some others started to erect crude shelters on the beach while some of the soldiers had rescued a chest of muskets from the waves – together with powder, balls and ramrods – and had managed to get some of the muskets to work, so they were sent up to the cliff top to hunt for game. 'And look for fresh water while you are there,' Jan had shouted after them. 'Our supply here is limited.'

A group of seamen were prising oysters off the rocks and others were making basic fish traps and scouring the rock pools for any edible creature. Everyone was hungry and, bit by bit, barrels of food that had survived the waves were dragged to safety and Annie made sure that the sick and wounded had first share of their contents. But all the remaining animals taken on at the Cape had perished so they would have no fresh meat unless they could shoot or trap it.

Late in the afternoon, two seamen came to her, triumphant. 'Look, mistress, what has been washed up,' they said.

Annie turned from persuading a man with a broken leg to take some fresh water. He was propped up against a rock, moaning and almost insensible. Annie had given him some brandy from one of the salvaged barrels, but his eyes were still staring with pain.

'Praise God,' she said, almost dropping the shell she was using as a scoop. 'The surgeon's box!'

With the men's help, she prised it open. The

contents were damp but there were, at least, some rolls of linen and bottles of medicines and some healing balm that had survived the waves, though some of the bottles had been smashed, their contents staining the linen.

She thanked the men and asked them to look out for anything else from the surgeon's cupboard.

'We can only take the goods that reach the water's edge, mistress,' said one. 'It is too dangerous to go further.'

Annie nodded. 'I know,' she said, seeing again the treacherous water between the ship and the shore. 'You have done well to save this, at least. It will give relief to several of the sick and wounded.'

She shouted to Lucas and he came to help her sort through the mess and salvage everything they could and, as they were squatting by the box, she asked, 'Where's my mother, Lucas? I've been so busy that I've not attended to her.'

'She's sitting over there, by the rock.' Lucas pointed to the far side of the beach.

'Keep sorting these, Lucas. I must go and see to her.'

When Annie reached Susan, she smiled with relief. Andries was at her breast again and this time he was sucking strongly. Annie squatted down beside them. 'Mother,' she said gently.

Susan looked up and smiled at her; she said nothing, but she stretched out and squeezed Annie's hand.

Chapter Twelve

Before sundown, all the survivors gathered together for a meal. The soldiers had shot two of the strange hopping creatures and their meat made tasty eating; and there were enough oysters and shellfish for most to have a taste, as well as supplies from the rescued barrels. The undermerchant, Jan Liebent, addressed them all as they ate.

'We shall not starve,' he announced. 'Because the ship was wrecked so close to the shore, many of the barrels from the hold have been salvaged. For the moment we have supplies of hams, cheeses, ship's biscuit, salted fish, wine and brandy, as well as some oil and butter. And, most importantly, water.'

'And what of tobacco?' shouted out one of the sailors.

Jan smiled. 'Aye. We have a goodly supply of tobacco and of clay pipes, too.'

There was a general murmuring of satisfaction and Jan held up his hand for silence.

'So, for now, we can survive.' He paused and looked around the assembled crowd. 'We are seventy-six souls here and if we are careful, we should make these supplies last for several weeks, especially if we can shoot more fresh meat and trap fish. However, our fresh water won't last long and we must set about finding another source.'

We may be seventy-six souls now, thought Annie, *but many of the injured will die.*

'And shall we be rescued?' asked one of the younger seamen.

Jan looked across at Melchior, who stood up.

'I have taken bearings,' he said. 'And I know our position. There will be other ships coming up this coast and we shall need to alert them to our presence.' He hesitated and Annie looked at François, who was sitting near Melchior. There was something in his expression that worried her. Why was he looking so glum? Surely, eventually they would be picked up by a passing ship? Melchior cleared his throat and went on:

'So, as soon as possible, we must make camp on the cliff top,' he said.

There were some murmurs of dissent. They had

just settled down on the beach; why should they uproot themselves?

'The seas here are unpredictable,' said Melchior, 'as you very well know. We cannot risk being washed away in further winter storms. And,' he continued, 'we need to be on the cliff top not only to be safe from the storms but also so that we can signal passing ships.' He paused. 'We shall keep a fire burning up there.'

'Thank you, Melchior,' said Jan, as Melchior sat down. 'The captain, the preacher, the surgeon and the other undermerchants have all perished and I am the only Company man among you, so I am in charge.' He gestured to Melchior and continued, 'I shall be assisted by the uppersteersman here and by the midshipmen and, in these dire straits, we shall expect every one of you to be as disciplined here as you would be on board ship.'

Annie looked about her. Already some of the rougher soldiers and seamen were eyeing her. She wasn't sure how Jan Liebent and the others would be able to restrain the men in such circumstances. She and her mother were the only women among the survivors.

God preserve us.

At that moment, François came to sit beside her and after all the others had disbursed, either to talk in groups or to try and settle to sleep, they stayed together as the fire burned low. Annie's thoughts turned again to May and she could no longer contain her tears.

'I miss her so much – what I would give to have her here!' She wiped her hand over her eyes. 'Perhaps she may yet be saved, François?'

François shook his head.

They were silent for a moment and then Annie asked, 'What will they do with the bodies, François?'

'The bodies will be burned, Annie,' he said quietly, scooping up a handful of sand and running it through his fingers.

She shuddered and moved closer to him. 'We've lost everything, yet we are alive.'

He nodded and then smiled. 'Not quite everything, Annie. One of my book clasps was washed ashore this afternoon.'

Annie put her hand up to the pouch hanging at her neck. 'The only thing I have is the tobacco box that Jacob gave me.' She paused, thinking back to her time working with Jacob, his kindness to her and his patient explanations. 'I wish to God he was here to help us now.'

François put his arm around her. 'He would have been proud of you, Annie. Your skill is already saving lives here.'

She leaned back into his embrace. 'What is to become of us, François?'

'Only God knows that, Annie, but, whatever happens, I swear on my life that I shall never leave you.'

A few days later, the *Zuytdorp* slipped beneath the waves and the only sign of that once-magnificent ship was the wreckage that continued to be spewed out on to the beach.

The survivors shifted their camp from the shore to the land on top of the cliffs. The cliffs behind the beach loomed over them but they were not insurmountable, and there was one place which was a gentler climb, though still difficult. Finally, a spot was selected on top of the cliffs some way inland from its edge, where there was shelter from rising ground.

Pieter Morreij, the ship's carpenter, was kept busy erecting more permanent shelters from timber and sailcloth, and Annie watched the men carry heavy supplies up the cliff, slipping and swearing as they lost their footing on the loose shale. Sailcloth, food, water, muskets and timbers were all dragged up, but the other wreckage was abandoned at the base of the cliff and some of the heavy barrels were stored in one of the shallow caves on the shore, though Jan was uneasy about this.

'They could be washed away in the next winter storm,' he said.

Eventually Annie, too, climbed up to the cliff top

camp. She had made sure that all the injured went before her, and it was a sorry sight to see them put over men's shoulders like so much baggage, or laid on makeshift stretchers. There was much moaning and groaning and sometimes sharp cries of pain as they were shunted up the cliff, often at a precarious angle and sometimes slipping from their bearers' grasp and tumbling backwards. But Jan and Melchior had made their decision and there were to be no exceptions. Everyone must stay together.

There were already many fewer of the sick and wounded; some had died, despite all Annie's ministrations, but a lot had recovered, too.

Once she had scrambled up the cliff, with Lucas and François helping her and Susan, she stood on the top and looked about her.

It was a desolate, hostile place, the rough sandy ground covered in boulders and scarred by deep fissures and holes. There were no trees or animals to be seen, and precious few birds; and there was dense, thorny scrub as far as the eye could see.

Annie shaded her eyes and stared inland towards the horizon. 'Dear God, it is an empty place,' she muttered.

'But it's safer up here, Annie,' said François. 'And there is some water, too.'

Annie frowned. 'Where?' she asked, looking about

her. Then François took her by the hand and led her over to a depression in the surface of the rock, which had filled with water. 'There are many of these over the surface,' said François. Annie stared down at it. 'Is that fresh?' she asked. François nodded and she knelt down beside the pool, scooped some water into her hands and drank it. Then she got to her feet, tearing her hand on a spiky plant as she did so. She gasped with pain and put her bleeding hand to her lips to suck at the blood.

'I hate it here,' she said. 'I knew Father's venture would end in disaster. Now he and May are gone and my mother is half mad with grief.' She turned to François, her eyes full. 'Will someone come for us, François? Shall we be rescued?'

François took her head in his hands. 'Of course we'll be rescued,' he said.

'But no one knows we are here, François. The VOC can't send a rescue ship from Java if they don't know where to look.'

'Didn't you hear what Melchior said?' replied François – and his tone was sharp, as it had been when he found her hiding in the hold. He continued. 'Ships pass this way on their way to the Indies. We shall light a beacon to alert them.'

'Not many ships will pass this way in winter, surely? You said yourself that it was too late in the season to take this route.'

François put his hands on her shoulders and shook her gently. 'Enough of this gloomy talk,' he said. 'We know that the *Belvliet* and the *Oostersteyn* are both coming along this route – and others. They will see us.' Then he turned and picked his way over the scrub and the scarred surface to join the other men.

Annie sniffed and rubbed her eyes. *He is as frightened as I am.*

But there was little time to worry about the future; the sick needed tending, as did her mother and baby brother. Susan was suckling the baby but she hardly ate or spoke; she was painfully thin and her eyes either darted nervously hither and thither or they were blank and unseeing. Annie and Susan were the only women left among the survivors and, although they had a small shelter to themselves, there was little privacy and with so few officers to defend them, they were vulnerable to the taunts and lewd comments from the rougher seamen and soldiers. It was difficult enough to survive, day by day, and to perform normal bodily functions, but Susan seemed unable to think for herself or keep herself or the baby clean, and needed always to be helped by Annie. Every day, Annie thought of May, yearning for her solid presence and her practical advice.

The days merged into one another and the group lived by the rising and setting of the sun; sometimes the skies were clear and sometimes the rains lashed their makeshift home and the wind howled about them so they were grateful for what little protection it afforded.

Then early one morning, François came running to them in a state of high excitement.

'Come out and look, Annie,' he said, hauling her up from where she was crouching, trying to wash the baby. She crawled out of the tent and stood up.

'There!' he said, pointing inland.

Annie frowned. 'What am I looking for?'

'A group of blacks,' he said. 'See, in the distance – and they are coming this way.'

Annie shaded her eyes and stared in the direction he was pointing and sure enough, in the haze of the early morning sun, she could see a shimmering movement. A group distorted by the light so that there was no telling how many they were or of what height or sex.

Instinctively, she touched the tobacco box at her throat.

'Melchior and I and some of the others will go out to meet them,' said François. He caught her hand. 'By God, Annie, this is good news. There are other humans in this accursed land. They will help us.'

Annie stared up at his eager face. 'Might they not kill us, François?'

He pretended not to hear her. 'I must go,' he said abruptly.

Annie stood where she was until she saw Melchior, François and a party of two or three others set off in the direction of the group of blacks. She noticed that a couple of soldiers at the rear of the party were armed with the salvaged muskets. She continued to watch anxiously and then, as Melchior's party came nearer, the blacks seemed to melt away. There was no obvious retreat, no noise or shouts, but suddenly they were no longer there. They had simply vanished.

They know this land so well, thought Annie. *They are a part of it and we are the intruders. We are out of place in this desolate country; we don't fit in. What must they think of us, with our strange clothes and our muskets?*

She turned to face the sea, then, and all its vast nothingness. There had been no sighting of a ship on the horizon, despite François's optimism.

They had only been in their new camp for a few days when the tension that had been brewing under the surface erupted. For some time now, there had been a hard core of discontented soldiers and seamen who had become more and more confident and insolent. They were already refusing to take orders from the few officers, sometimes laughing in their faces. Melchior and Jan were doing their best, but their threats of naval discipline rang hollow. The men knew, as well as the officers, that their chances of rescue were slim and that the VOC no longer ruled their lives.

Most of the supplies of brandy and wine were in the barrels down on the shore and, one night, Annie awoke to hear shouting and singing coming from the base of the cliff. Nervously, she crept out of her makeshift tent; she was not alone. The noise had awakened most of those left above and she saw Melchior, with Jan and the other midshipmen, talking in low voices. She went over to them.

'What's happening?' she asked.

François saw her but he didn't smile. 'Some of the men have broached the wine and brandy barrels,' he said.

'What can you do?'

Melchior replied. 'There are too many of them and too few of us. We'll leave them for now. I doubt any of them will make it back up the cliff tonight and they'll have sore heads in the morning.'

But he was wrong. Later in the night Annie woke again to hear sounds outside her tent – drunken guffaws and lewd, slurred comments.

'I'll have that little wench in there, see if I don't,' said one of the men.

'And I'll have her next.'

'And I'll have her mother.'

Terrified, Annie sat up and tried to think. It was dark and the tent was small; there was no way in which she and Susan could escape. Her mother stirred beside her and she could sense her fear. She reached out for Susan's arm.

'Scream, Mother! It's our only hope.'

And Annie screamed, then, with all her might. A raw, primeval noise that came from deep within her. It startled the baby and he joined in and, eventually, Susan started to wail, too. Momentarily, the laughter and drunken comments outside stopped, but then three or four men burst in, tripping over, lunging at the women.

'François!' yelled Annie, as one of the men put a rough hand over her mouth and pressed her back down on the ground. Another of them was already attacking her mother, when someone came in from behind them.

It was not François who was first on the scene but Pieter Morreij, the carpenter, wielding a stout plank of wood and cracking skulls with it. He was a big strong man and, unlike the assailants, he was sober and his blows were accurate.

'Get off her, you drunken lout,' he yelled at the man on top of Annie and the man rolled to one side, holding his head and yelping with pain. Then one of the other seamen grabbed Pieter from behind and tried to wrestle him to the ground. Annie's attacker seized his chance and came back at her. She fought him with screams and scratches. 'Little vixen,' he said, his breath foul and his words slurred. 'I like a girl who fights.' Susan was faring no better and two of the men were holding her down. Pieter fended off his attacker and came to Susan's aid, raining blows on heads and backs and shouting at the men.

Then, at last, more help arrived. Melchior, Jan, François and others crashed through the scrub and entered the tent, dragging the men off Susan and Annie and forcing them outside.

François stayed inside with the women, who were both sobbing with fright.

'I'm so sorry,' he said, his own voice breaking. 'I should have guarded you against this.'

Annie wiped her eyes with the back of her hand. 'How could you protect us?' she asked, sniffing. 'There are too many of them. It will happen again.'

'Of course it won't happen again,' said François. 'These men will be severely punished, you can be sure of that.'

'How? How can you punish them?' Her voice was angry now. 'We are in a barren wilderness here, François. They don't care any more. They are sure they will die and they want to take what they can while they still live. They may have been afraid of punishment when they were on board ship, but it is different here.'

'They will be punished when we are rescued . . .' began François, but Annie turned away from him, exasperated. 'You stupid boy,' she muttered. 'How can you think we'll ever be rescued?'

For the rest of the night, François and Pieter slept outside the women's tent and in the early morning there was a gloomy silence about the campsite. Annie, her mother and the baby did not wake as early as usual and it was François who roused Annie.

When he shook her arm, she sat up immediately, batting him away, her eyes wide with fear until she saw who it was. 'Oh God, François, how you frightened me. I thought it was them again.'

He smiled at her. 'You need have no more fear of that drunken mob,' he said. 'They've gone.'

She frowned. 'What do you mean, gone?'

'They must have left before dawn,' he said. 'They've taken a goodly supply of food and other goods – and even one of the muskets – but they have left the camp.'

'How many?'

'About twenty are missing,' he said.

'But where will they go? How will they survive?'

François shrugged. 'We think they may have gone looking for native tribes, to make a home with them.'

'And what does Jan Liebent say about this?'

François sat down on the ground and stretched his legs in front of him. 'He is relieved that some of the troublemakers are gone, but he is angry, too. It will look bad for him, when we are rescued, that his discipline was too lax to control the men.'

Annie was about to voice her doubts about being rescued when Susan stirred and reached for the sleeping Andries, to feed him. Annie looked across at them – and back at François. 'She is not well, François,' she whispered. 'She is wasting away and her mind wanders. She mutters to herself and to the baby, but when I speak to her she doesn't respond any more. And the horror of last night . . .'

For the next few days, Annie lived in fear that the drunken crew members would return and attack her, but there was no sign of them. The small group of survivors on top of the cliff worked harder, now, to forage for food, keep the fire lit and see to their daily needs.

Melchior and Jan were trying to establish a routine and they had renewed the custom of morning prayers. There was something comforting about saying the familiar words in this wild place, while the waves crashed below them.

After prayers, as Jacob had in the past, Annie would take Lucas with her as she made her rounds of the sick and wounded, but there was not so much to occupy them now. There were always sores and cuts to attend to and splinters to draw out, but those with broken limbs had either died or were shuffling about on rough crutches made by Pieter, and those who had not died of disease were gradually recovering. Her main concern, now, was for her poor deranged mother, but she also turned her attention to Lucas again, and sometimes they would climb down the cliff to the beach below and she would watch him writing his letters in the sand. Often, after this, they would go back to the wreck site and every day there were more items washed ashore; mostly smaller items now – belt buckles, keys, bowls, an iron ring, a side-plate, buttons, clay pipes, glass goblets and silver coins. And many, many more coins out of reach, lying on the surface of the rock beneath the waves, a carpet of silver, glinting sometimes when the water was clear.

Often, now, when they reached the top of the cliff with their booty, they would glimpse a group of blacks in the distance and once, quite nearby, standing off, watching them. But every time Melchior and the others made to go and greet them, they melted away. Jan Liebent was getting frustrated.

'We need to make contact with them,' he said. 'We must find a reliable source of water before the summer comes. Our supplies won't last long and the water in these rock pools will dry up.'

The summer, thought Annie. *Dear God, shall we still be in this cursed place in the summer?*

Melchior was thoughtful. 'We have had no success

in approaching them. Perhaps we should wait for them to come to us?'

Jan scowled. 'What if they never do? What then?'

Melchior shrugged. Jan irritated him. He was tired of the man and wished to God they'd not been thrown together in this way.

But all animosity was put aside a few days later when there was a shout from one of the seamen.

'A ship, sir. A ship, on the horizon!'

Chapter Thirteen

The cry echoed round the campsite and people ran towards the edge of the cliff, dropping what they were doing, emerging from their shelters, all surging forward to look, to make sure the man had not imagined it.

But he was right – it was there, a ghostly outline creeping along the horizon.

'Build up the fire.'

Everyone helped, scurrying hither and thither. Piles of the thorny scrub bushes were pulled up and heaped on to the blaze, together with anything that would burn – driftwood, chests, ship's furniture – until the fire was a huge roaring beacon.

Surely they will notice us, thought Annie.

They all stood, then, staring out to sea, willing the ship to slow in its passage, to turn towards them.

'What sort of ship is she?' one of the men asked Melchior. 'Is she a VOC ship?'

He shook his head. 'I can't tell. She's too far away for me to identify.'

They waited in silence. The only noise now was the crackling of the fire and the breaking of the waves on the shore below.

'They must be able to see the fire,' said someone. 'Aye,' said another, 'but they may think it is a native fire. Why should they think otherwise? No one knows we are here.'

Slowly, steadily, smoothly, the ship slid out of sight and gradually the defeated survivors went back to their tasks.

'If only the cannon were not lost,' said Melchior.

It was a gloomy party that night that ate their meal by the fire. At last, Jan Liebent stood up and addressed them.

'It seems we are unlikely to be rescued until the better weather comes,' he said. There was a long pause and he added quietly, 'And maybe not even then.' There were some mutterings among the men but no one contradicted him. 'So we must redouble our efforts to make contact with the natives.'

'They know we are here,' said Melchior. 'Maybe it is better we wait –'

Jan cut him short. 'No. We must seek them out;

we must send out parties daily. We urgently need to contact them.'

However, just as the first party was being sent out the following morning, a large group of blacks was sighted not far off. Jan urged his men to go and meet them but Melchior restrained them. 'They are coming to us, this time,' he said to Jan. 'They are much nearer. I beg you to wait. Stay here and see what happens. I am convinced that they are frightened when we go to seek them out.'

'Nonsense, man,' said Jan. But, as the tribesmen came closer, he waited, as Melchior had advised.

The blacks advanced slowly and quietly on the camp and came to a halt a short distance from its edge. No one moved except Jan, who made to go forward. Melchior put a restraining hand on his arm. 'Wait, man,' he hissed. 'Wait, I beg you.'

The two groups – the survivors from the wreck and the native tribe – stared at each other. Lucas was standing next to Annie and she grabbed his arm, digging her nails into his flesh as she stared at the unfamiliar sight. They were mostly naked, though some had strings at their waists and skins over their shoulders. The men were armed with spears and shields and, after a while, a few of these advanced a little nearer the campsite while the rest of the party stayed back. Slowly, tentatively, Jan and Melchior took a few steps forward and, when the blacks did not retreat, they advanced further. Annie and the others watched, hardly daring to breathe. She noticed that a couple of the soldiers had their muskets close to hand but they did not pick them up.

No one in the company broke the silence as Jan and Melchior came closer to the native men until at last they were face to face. Melchior slowly lowered himself to sit on the ground and spread out his hands in a gesture of submission. Awkwardly, Jan did the same, though, even at a distance, Annie could sense his unease at relinquishing his authority. The native men stayed standing, looking first at the two men in front of them and then beyond them at the people assembled at the camp. The men were silent, but the others – the crowd behind them – were not. They were chatting and pointing at all the things which must have been so unfamiliar to them. The sailcloth, the clothes of the seamen and soldiers which, although tattered now, were so strange and unsuited to the terrain. Some of the women in the party were pointing at Annie and at Susan and giggling behind their hands.

Then, an older man in the front party sat down on the ground across from Melchior and Jan, and the others did the same. Melchior beckoned François to come over to them. 'Fetch food,' he said quietly.

François and one or two others collected a

supply of ship's biscuit and took it over. Only the old tribesman tasted it and he soon spat it out on the ground. Annie couldn't help smiling. 'I don't blame him,' she whispered to Lucas. 'It's hard as iron and just as tasteless.'

For a long time, then, Jan and Melchior were engaged in some form of communication with what Annie took to be the tribal chiefs. At one point, she saw Jan making gestures of drinking and wondered whether his request for a water source would be understood. Then, after a while, Jan and Melchior rose to their feet and made sweeping gestures with their arms to invite the tribe to come nearer, into the heart of the camp, and to sit by the fire.

Tentatively, at first, they came forward. The men with their spears and shields, followed by the others. There were some children among them and Annie wondered what they were doing. Surely they wouldn't take young children on a hunting party? Perhaps the whole group were on their way to another camp?

She stared at them. They were quite different from the natives they had seen in the Gulf of Guinea or at the Cape; their noses broader, their faces wider and their hair less tightly curled. She watched as some of the older men crouched down and examined the ground minutely. Jan, Melchior and some of the soldiers and sailors brought goods for them to look at; goblets, belt buckles, coins. At first, the men just stared at the objects, then they touched them and eventually picked them up, one by one, smelt them, bit them and then discarded them.

'They have no need of such stuff,' said Lucas.

Annie nodded, but she wasn't listening. She had seen a young woman holding a baby of about Andries's age. She turned to Susan who was standing silently, close beside her, grasping her arm.

'I'm going to take Andries over to those women, Mother.'

Susan stared at her, saying nothing. Gently, Annie pulled her arm from Susan's grasp and went into their tent. Andries was awake, gurgling on his rough bed, kicking his legs in the air. Annie bent down and picked him up, crawled out of the tent and then straightened up.

Even before she approached the women in the group of natives, they had spotted him and were making clucking noises and clapping their hands together. Annie took him over to them and sat down with the women. They all wanted to touch him, chatting among themselves, giggling and stroking his pale skin, so different from theirs. Fortunately, this didn't seem to frighten Andries and he continued to gurgle. The women touched Annie, too, fingering the cloth of her skirt and the remaining buttons on it and then unwinding the linen in which she had wrapped Andries. Annie tried to keep still and show no fear though, in truth, she was very uncomfortable with dark hands tugging and stroking her. And their smell was so different; smoke and sweat mixed with a sharp aromatic scent she could not identify. She would smell foul to them, too, no doubt. She had been in the same clothes ever since the *Zuytdorp* ran aground and she had hardly washed herself since then.

The young woman with her own baby was particularly fascinated by Andries and Annie handed him to her to hold and took the woman's baby in exchange. They smiled at each other, pointing and gesturing. Then the little native baby started to cry and the girl gave Andries back and put her own baby to her breast to feed.

I must find something to give her, thought Annie. Slowly, she got to her feet, holding Andries to her, and went to fetch some buttons and some of the other trinkets she had salvaged from the wreck. When she came back with them, the women took them, smelt them and then bit them, in the same way that their menfolk had done. The buttons were the only things that seemed to interest them.

As Annie was bending over, showing them the buttons, one of the women reached forward and held on to the pouch around her neck. Annie took it off and opened it up, showing her Jacob's brass tobacco box inside. This seemed to intrigue her, particularly the depiction of the town of Leyden on its lid. She pointed at the drawing of the houses and spires and chatted excitedly. Gently, Annie took it back from the women. It was one possession she was not ready to part with.

There was some movement among the men. The three or four older natives who had been with Jan and Melchior had now risen and were making ready to depart – and they were gesturing for the survivors to follow them.

Jan made a decision. 'I think,' he said to those within earshot, 'that they are saying that they will show us where there is water.'

Melchior nodded. 'If that's the case, then some of us should go with them,' he said. He looked about him. 'François, get a group of four or five strong young men and follow the natives. Quickly, now, before they disappear. Who knows when we'll see them again.'

François nodded and chose four others to go with him. He had no chance to say goodbye to Annie, for the natives were moving off. Although they all walked away from the camp together, when they had gone a little way, four of the natives and François and his group broke away and headed to the south. The rest of the natives went north and Annie stood looking after them, thinking of the young woman whose baby she had cradled as they disappeared into the distance.

François and his companions didn't return that evening, nor were they there the next morning, but Jan didn't seem worried.

'If they are taking them to a water source, it may be some way distant,' he said.

But Annie was frantic and all through the next day she kept staring towards the south, willing him to reappear. When night fell she was fretting, too, about her mother. Susan would do nothing to help herself now. She spent the day rocking to and fro, moaning, and she even appeared to have lost interest in the baby. Annie had to put him to her mother's breast, otherwise he would have had no nourishment.

For the hundredth time, she wished that Jacob had been there to advise her. Cuts, bruises, broken limbs and diseases, she understood. But she had no idea what to do about a broken mind. That night, Annie hardly slept, imagining that François had been attacked by the natives and thinking of the future, too – of what she could do if her mother stopped nursing the baby and whether they would all die from lack of water when summer came.

Then, very early the next morning, she woke to the sound of laughter and cheering. Quickly, she scrambled out of her tent to see François and his companions talking to Jan and Melchior. François saw her and beckoned her to come over. She ran over to him, resisting the urge to fling herself into his arms.

'The Lord be praised, Annie,' said Melchior, grinning broadly. 'They are returned unharmed – and with some good news.'

Annie noticed two native spears lying on the ground and Melchior followed her gaze. 'They were a gift, were they not, François?'

'Aye,' said François. 'The natives took us down to the shore and they showed us how they spear fish, and,' he continued, 'they took us to a water-soak south-east of our campsite and an easy day's walk from here and they showed us how to make fire from the strange "grass" trees that grow hereabouts and how to eat the starch from its stems. And they caught a small dragon and roasted it on their fire – and gave us snails and grubs, to eat, too.'

Annie looked up at François's animated face. 'And you learnt all this without being able to speak to them?'

He laughed. 'Aye, it is strange how much can be said without speech – we talked through gestures, through expressions – and I began to recognize some of the sounds they made, too –'

Melchior interrupted him. 'Well done, boy. If we can learn to communicate with the natives then we may survive.' Then he looked serious. 'All this is good, François, but we also need to think to the future, to the months ahead.'

Jan Liebent frowned. 'What do you mean, Melchior? We can stay here, can we not? One day a passing ship will see us.'

Melchior took Jan's arm and led him a little way apart from the others. Annie and François watched as they spoke in low voices and they could only catch an occasional word. 'No, you are wrong, Melchior. There's no need.' And again. 'No, I say.' And finally, Jan walked off angrily, saying, 'You forget who is in charge, man.'

François was still standing close to Annie. He bent down and whispered in her ear, 'I wish to God they got on better.'

Annie nodded. 'I would sooner Melchior was in charge than Jan,' she said. 'He is the one who understands charts and can read the stars.'

'Aye,' said François. 'He's a good man to have by you when you are lost.'

'And Jan's no seaman,' continued Annie, 'he's just a Company man. He's only worried about what will happen to the Company's cargo; he doesn't care about the people.'

'Don't be so hard on him, Annie. When we get to Java, he will have to take the blame for what has happened to the Company's property.'

'When we get to Java,' repeated Annie. 'Shall we ever reach Java, François?'

François lowered himself to the ground and motioned for Annie to sit beside him.

'Maybe,' he said quietly. 'If Melchior gets his way.' He paused. 'It's a dilemma, Annie. Jan wants to be close to the Company's property, so it can be guarded and anything that floats ashore can be salvaged, but if we stay here then no one will be able to rescue us.' He swept his arm around the cliffs. 'No ship can come in here to anchor and even if Pieter the carpenter could build us a boat from driftwood, we could never launch it here – the seas are far too treacherous.'

Annie sighed impatiently. 'So what is to be done? Does Melchior have a plan?'

François nodded. 'Melchior is a steersman,' he said quietly. 'He has studied the charts and he knows more about this coastline than Jan – than any of us. And he does have a plan.'

Annie's eyes opened wide.

François plucked a twig from the brittle, spiky bush beside him. 'He told me of it, but he wants Jan Liebent to agree to it. He does not want to cause a rift between the two of them.'

'And what *is* it?'

François cleared his throat. 'There's a great river to the south of here; he pointed it out to us as we passed it on the *Zuytdorp*, so I've seen it with my own eyes. It is where the two men from the ship *Batavia* were marooned some eighty years ago.'

'And does he want us to go to this river?' asked Annie.

François nodded. 'He wants to send out an advance party to find it and to see if there is a place where we could establish a more permanent camp on its banks so that we would always have plentiful water – and food.' He looked down at the ground. 'And there, maybe, we could build some sort of seaworthy vessel and set sail for Java.'

Annie was silent, thinking of her mother and baby Andries.

How could they survive such a journey?

François continued. 'But Jan doesn't want to leave here. He frets over all that Company silver spilt out and lying beneath the surface.'

Annie remembered the blacks biting the pieces of silver. She smiled. 'The natives would have no use for it, surely?'

François shrugged. 'I think Jan is terrified to strike out for the unknown. He doesn't want to leave a place where we have food and shelter.'

Annie frowned. 'But surely, if he sent a small party and then they came back and reported to him . . .'

'But Melchior would insist on being part of the

advance party and Jan Liebent does not want to be left here without him.'

Annie looked up at François. 'And you, François? Would you want to be part of such an advance party?'

He nodded. 'Melchior has already asked me to accompany him – if he can persuade Jan.' He paused. 'That is why he was so ready to send me with the natives to find a water source and to observe how they live and what can be safely eaten.'

Annie stared at his eager face. 'You said you would never leave me, François,' she said softly, already knowing that she could not stop him going.

He took her hands in his then. 'And I won't, Annie. If I join Melchior's party, it is so that we can find a better place where we can be together – and a place from which we have a chance to escape.'

Annie could feel the tears coming to her eyes and she looked away and out to sea.

Everyone deserts me, she thought. *My father, May and now François. And I am left in charge of a demented mother and a helpless baby.*

Chapter Fourteen

At dawn a few days later, the advance party finally set off. Jan Liebent was not happy about it and it had taken all Melchior's powers of persuasion to leave with his blessing. Annie could understand why Jan was unhappy. The advance party consisted of Melchior, Pieter the carpenter, François, two seamen, two soldiers and Lucas.

Annie was horrified that they were taking Lucas with them. 'He's only a boy,' she said to François.

'Aye, he may be only a boy,' replied François, 'but he is fit and strong and willing. And,' he added, 'it seems that Melchior has a soft spot for a lad who is so eager for adventure.'

It is my doing, thought Annie. *If I had not treated his sores and made sure he was better fed he wouldn't be the strong lad he is today*. And she might have added that she was responsible for building his confidence, too.

'Is this really what you want, Lucas?' she had asked him.

'It is an honour to be asked, Mistress Annie,' he said. 'Though I shall be sad to leave you behind.'

Annie smiled. 'You will be very useful to the group.'

'And I know most of my letters,' he said, grinning. Annie couldn't help but smile in response. Knowledge of his letters would be of little help to him in this hostile terrain.

The group was loaded down with whatever they could carry; some food and water, a musket and one of the native spears, and the precious tinderbox.

Jan was losing seven strong men and a lad. He was losing the master carpenter and the uppersteersman – but Melchior had insisted that the carpenter accompany them, arguing that only Pieter could advise on the best place for making a permanent camp. 'I can read the tides and the winds, Jan, but I do not know, as Pieter does, how to build good shelters and with what materials, or whether the ground is suitable. We need him with us.'

Jan's reluctance to allow the men to leave the camp was understandable. And, most of all, thought Annie, he would miss the strength, wisdom and expertise of Melchior. As would they all.

François had a few private moments with Annie before he left.

'Don't worry about me, Annie. I shall be in good company and Melchior will guide us. And, if we follow the coast south then we are sure to reach the great river. There really is little danger.'

'Little danger! God in heaven, François. You have no idea what else might be in the wild places.'

He laughed. 'I know there are the strange hopping creatures and the little dragons, but we can eat them, Annie.'

'And the snakes, François.'

He looked serious for a moment; one of the soldiers had died from a snake bite. 'Aye. You are right. We must be on the lookout for snakes.'

Annie held him tight and gazed up at his animated face. It was such an adventure for him. 'God go with you, François. I will pray for you all.'

Then, just as he was turning away from her, she said, 'Will you not say goodbye to my mother?'

François squatted at Susan's side and took her hand, but she snatched it away and shuffled sideways, muttering.

'God knows how long she can survive like this,' said Annie softly.

François got to his feet. 'She is sure to survive,' he said confidently. 'For she has the best nurse in the world.'

A little later, all the remaining survivors gathered to say goodbye to Melchior, François, Lucas and the others and wish them Godspeed though, as they watched them leave, there was an unspoken dread among all those left behind that they might be seeing them for the last time.

Annie waited until the group had disappeared among the scrub and vanished from sight, before she turned back to see to her mother and baby brother.

A gloom settled over the camp after the group's departure and Annie was as affected by the atmosphere as everyone else. She had no real friends among the survivors now, and communication with her mother was impossible. Most of her time was spent in trying to persuade her to eat and making sure that Andries got some nourishment from her.

The baby was her only joy and she delighted in him. Although he was still so young, his personality was beginning to develop and despite all his privations and the misery of their circumstances, he was a cheerful little soul, gurgling and smiling and holding out his arms to her when she approached. Often she would strap him to her front, as she had done on that terrifying night on board the Zuytorp, and see to the sick or do other tasks with Andries as her companion. She loved to feel the warmth of his little body close to her and the reassurance of his regular heartbeat.

And at night, as he lay between her and her mother, she would sing songs to him to get him off to sleep or tell him the stories that Susan had told her when she was little. He would have no understanding of them, of course, but she hoped that their familiarity might stimulate Susan; occasionally, when she did this, Susan would focus on Annie and smile at her, but her silences were becoming longer and more profound.

Jan Liebent's temper had not improved. Annie understood that he was worried – how could he not be? Worried about the precious cargo, about the absence of some of his best men and worried, too, that his authority would, once again, be questioned and more of the survivors would desert him. But there was such an apathy and resignation among the remaining survivors that it seemed unlikely that anyone would have had the energy to leave. Their hopes were pinned on the little group travelling south to find them a place where they could set up a safer and more permanent camp – and from which they could, perhaps, escape and sail to Java.

The days passed, the routines continued, although the supplies from the ship were dwindling and the remaining men had to hone their fishing skills and hunt more of the animals which lived on the cliff top.

Annie began to help with gutting and cooking

fish and often, when she was doing this, her thoughts turned to May and her romance with the other Jan, the cook on the *Zuytdorp*. She wondered where he was now; was he still on the island in the Gulf of Guinea? Had he survived?

And daily, as she worked, she prayed for the safety of Melchior and the others – but particularly for that of François and Lucas.

Although the days merged into one another and no one kept a record of dates, it must have been about a week after François and the others had left that Annie awoke one morning to find the place next to her empty. Her mother had gone.

Annie picked up Andries and went out to look for her. At first she thought that Susan had simply wandered off into the scrub to relieve herself, but there was no sign of her in her customary spots. Annie questioned everyone else she saw but no one had seen Susan. At last one of the midshipmen who had been up earlier than the others said he thought he'd seen her heading for the edge of the cliff.

'What! Did you not stop her?' said Annie, angrily.

The young man shrugged. 'I did not want to disturb her,' he said lamely. 'She has a right to gaze out to sea, does she not?'

Annie headed for the cliff edge and looked down

at the shore below, but there was no sign of Susan and her stomach cramped with fear. Susan had never done this before. She went to Jan Liebent and told him but he showed little interest.

'Where would she go, Annie?' said Jan. 'She wouldn't wander off into the scrub. And surely she'd not desert the baby. She'll be back soon.' And with that he turned away and continued to give some instructions to a group of men who were about to set off to fish. When he'd finished and the men made to leave, Annie said to one of them, 'I'll come with you. It may be that my mother is down on the shore.'

The men helped Annie as she slipped and slithered her way down the cliff face, trying to keep upright with Andries strapped to her chest. The remaining men at the camp were kind to her, on the whole, and she'd had none of the trouble she'd encountered earlier from the rougher soldiers and seamen – those who had deserted and struck off on their own.

When at last they reached the bottom of the cliff, the men went further along the coast to fish, to a spot where the natives had shown them, and Annie started to look up and down the beach. She stayed at the wreck site for a few moments, trying to think where her mother might go and, as she looked towards the place where the *Zuytdorp* had sunk, she marvelled at how the sea had reclaimed the great ship. There was no sign of it now, and the glint of silver beneath the water on the broad shelf of rock was the only clue to all the wealth she had carried.

Andries started to grizzle and Annie kissed the top of his head.

'I know, baby. You must be hungry. We'll find her, then you shall have your milk.'

Annie started her search in the caves; there were still a few barrels stored in them but, although she called and called, there was no answering cry and no trace of her mother, so she scrambled round the point and to the south where their first camp had been.

The place was deserted, the only sign that there had been a camp here was a circle of ash where they had made their fire, well above the waterline, and some scraps of sailcloth snared on a sharp rock.

Annie stood helplessly at the base of the cliff. She was sure that Susan was not at the camp above, yet she didn't appear to be here either. Surely she would not have gone wandering off into the scrub on her own? But then, would she really have climbed down the cliff on her own?

Her fear mounting, Annie decided to go further along the coast to the fishing place but, just as she was turning away, she noticed something. There was a big pool of seawater obscured from view by an outcrop of rock and as the sun shone down from a cloudless sky,

Annie saw a scrap of something caught in its glare at the very edge of the pool, which was all that was visible to her from where she stood.

Very carefully, she made her way over the sharp rock, scraping her bare feet and nearly losing her balance as Andries struggled against her until at last she could see the pool more clearly. She stopped abruptly and clasped Andries tight.

Susan was lying face down in the water, her skirts weighing her down, her body moving from side to side as the waves came in and out of the rock pool.

Annie struggled forward, no longer feeling the sharp cuts on her feet.

'Dear God,' she whispered. 'Dear God, please let her be alive.'

Annie ran into the water but when she reached Susan, she couldn't move her.

'Mother,' she screamed. And her cry was so harsh that Andries started to yell.

For what seemed like an eternity, Annie stood there looking down on her mother's lifeless body. She didn't heed the water lapping at her knees or the tide pulling at her and it was only when Andries began to yell in earnest that, automatically, she tried to comfort him.

'Oh baby, what shall I do?' she whispered as she rocked him to and fro. 'How will you survive without her? How shall I?'

At last, she struggled out of the water and back over the rocks and ran, the baby jiggling up and down, further on to the place where the men were fishing. They looked up as they saw her approach, sensing her distress. One of them came to meet her.

'What is it, mistress?'

Annie could hardly speak from the running. 'My mother, it's my mother!' They abandoned the fishing and she led them back to the rock pool. Between them, the men managed to lift Susan from the water and carry her back to the base of the cliff. When they laid her down on the sand, Annie bent over her, kissing her cold face. She took one of Susan's hands in hers and gently unbent her mother's fingers. In the palm of the loosened hand lay a button and Annie picked it up and looked at it.

She could hold back her sobs no longer. The men let her weep and one of them took Andries from her and rocked him gently in his arms.

When the sobs had eased a little, Annie took the baby back from the man. She showed Andries the button.

'This was your father's,' she whispered.

The men helped Annie back up the cliff to the camp and they went to report what had happened to Jan Liebent.

'I'm sorry to hear that, Annie, but it was probably

for the best. She was in a sorry state, was she not?'

Annie could not speak for anger. How could the death of her mother be for the best? She might have recovered her senses, mightn't she? Who was to tell? And what would happen to Andries now? How was he to survive? She knew that there was no point in asking the question of Jan. A weak baby was of no concern to him and no doubt he thought the best thing, for all concerned, was to let Andries die.

Later in the day, some of the men built a fire at the base of the cliff and burned Susan's body. Annie could not bear to go down to witness it.

'Forgive me, Mother,' she said. 'I cannot be at your burning.' But she and Andries stood at the cliff top and watched the fire from a distance, seeing the flames leaping into the still sky and, when Annie could watch no longer, she turned back to their empty tent. And as she walked back, Annie whispered to the baby, 'I do not know how I can achieve it, Andries, but I swear to you that I will do everything in my power to save you.'

But how? There was no one to help her now. All she could do was to try and keep the baby alive with water and with mushed-up scraps of food, but he would not take any of the food she offered him; he even spat out the boiled rice she made for him. By the end of that day, she was at her wits' end.

'You need your mother's milk, baby, don't you,' she

muttered to him as she cradled the grizzling baby in her arms. 'And I cannot supply it for you.' As darkness fell, she went to find Jan Liebent. He was sitting beside the fire, talking to one of the midshipmen. He looked up briefly as she approached but then ignored her and continued to speak to the man. Annie did not move. She continued to stand beside him, observing how thin he had become and how wild looking, with a great shaggy beard on him. Eventually, when Andries's grizzles continued, he looked at her again and frowned. 'Yes?' he said shortly.

Annie swallowed. 'Forgive me, sir –' she began.

'Yes, yes – what is it, child? You can see I am occupied.'

Annie fought back her anger. Child, indeed!

'Sir, I need to find nourishment for the baby. I thought to –'

She got no further. Jan held up a hand to silence her. 'For God's sake, mistress, this is no place for a babe. He will not survive without his mother; let him go.'

Annie's head jerked up. 'Let him go? How dare you say that! He is my brother, sir. The last survivor of my family – and I will not let him die.' She went on, falling over her words in her distress. 'There is a native girl who could help us; I saw her suckling her infant. If I could find her . . . if you could release one of your men to accompany me . . .'

Jan laughed harshly. 'What a foolish notion, girl. We have no idea where the natives are camped. They move about all the time. To try and find them would be impossible – and I would certainly not release any of my men to go on such a wild errand. They are all needed here. Let the child pass away peacefully; it will be better for all concerned.'

Fighting back her tears, Annie turned away and, as she did so, she caught the eye of the young midshipman; but she knew he would never disobey orders, even if she begged him to help her.

Annie lay awake for most of that night, the baby fretful beside her and, before dawn broke, she had made her decision. Silently, she gathered up what she needed, creeping around the camp, taking a little food and some water and then, strapping Andries securely to her chest, she slipped out of the camp and headed north, just as the first light was streaking the sky.

She told no one of her plans. In her mind's eye was the picture of the nursing native mother who had come to the camp earlier and had delighted in the sight of Andries.

'It's our only chance, Andries,' she whispered to the baby. 'If we can find their camp, then maybe she will agree to feed you as well as her own baby.'

Chapter Fifteen

Annie went as fast as she was able, encumbered as she was by the baby and slowed up by the scrubby bushes which snared her clothes, and the rock-strewn soil beneath her feet. Her feet! She had been wearing shoes when she jumped from the *Zuytdorp*'s rigging, but they had soon come off with the force of the water. She and most of the other survivors had had to improvise their footwear from driftwood and leather straps, but she had been lucky to find some shoes washed ashore and, although they didn't match – or fit – they gave her a little protection from the rough ground. When May was alive they had both sewn clothes and Annie fondly remembered so many times when they were both bent over their work, stitching and gossiping.

Annie looked down at her soiled skirt. Once she had

been proud of her appearance – and although there had been precious little room on board ship, she had had a silk dress with her, and stays, too. But they had learnt – she, May and Susan – to dispense with such frippery in the tropics and had worn simple garments, which were less heavy. Although there'd been little enough choice on board, there was no choice at all here. Some of the seamen had fashioned rough needles from fish bones and thread from animal gut to do simple repairs, but Annie had never found these clumsy implements satisfactory and longed for her own needles and thread. Her skirt and bodice hung about her now; she was much thinner and she fancied she had grown taller, too.

When she was out of sight of the camp, she slowed down and took a small sip from the water bottle slung around her neck. As she reached for it, she felt the pouch and clutched it.

'Why did you do it, Jacob? Why did you leave us, when we needed you so badly?'

The bush around her was stirring, and she stopped and listened. How had she ever thought that this place was deserted? There were subtle noises all around her, birds wheeling and screeching on the sea's edge, the scuttling and buzzing of insects and, once, she almost trod on one of the furry hopping animals before it jumped up from its resting place and bounded away from her, making her stumble in alarm. She tried to keep a lookout for snakes, too, as she forged her way in between the dense scrub, and she did see one once, slithering away from her. Sometimes she would come upon animal tracks to follow, but they crisscrossed the ground and were narrow and often petered out.

She tried to get Andries to take a little water but he resisted her. Already he was becoming weak and listless; it was more than a day and a night since he'd tasted his mother's milk.

'Please take some water, baby,' she whispered. 'It will keep you alive.'

But Andries just grizzled and spat out the water.

As they drew further away from the campsite, the going became harder. The bushes were taller and more dense and there were deep, wide fissures in the rock face, impossible to cross, meaning that to keep going north, with the sea on her left hand, Annie frequently had to walk due east to the end of these deep gullies before heading north again.

By noon, she was exhausted. She found a place to sit in the shade of a bush and brought out the dried fish and cheese and a little of the soft rice she had tried to tempt Andries with earlier. While she ate she tried again to force the rice into the baby's mouth but he only choked and it ran down his chin. She opened his toothless gums with her fingers and trickled some water down his throat. Taken by surprise, he swallowed enough to moisten his mouth, at least, before choking and crying again.

'Hush, Andries,' Annie said. 'You must drink.'

Wearily, she stood up and started stumbling forward again though, as Jan Liebent had pointed out, there was no knowing where the natives were camped. Maybe when the native women had visited the survivors' camp they were only passing and were going to some much further settlement. Maybe they weren't going due north, as it had seemed, but somewhere inland. She frowned. Why had she so recklessly embarked on this venture?

Perhaps, after all, there was something of her father in her. For sure, he'd been reckless to bring them on this journey, a journey with so many disasters and so much delay, but how could any of them have known that a year on from when they set out from Zeeland with such high hopes, she and a new baby would be the only ones left alive? Her father had risked everything for the promise of a job in the East, but perhaps she was as bad – as reckless – forsaking the relative safety of the camp to strike out on her own in a land full of hazards she didn't understand.

She started talking to Andries. 'I thought it for the best, Andries. But now I have no idea where we are going or if we shall ever find the natives' camp.'

They had been following the line of a particularly

long gully and now they were a long way from the sea, and the gully still stretched ahead of them. Annie plodded on, her arms aching and her legs scratched and bleeding. At last the gully ended but by this time she had lost all sense of direction. She stopped and looked about her; the gully had wound and wiggled its way inland and she couldn't be sure that she was still heading north. She squinted up at the sun, trying to gauge her direction from it, but it was almost directly overhead so, until the day wore on and it began to sink, it would be no help to her.

She had to keep stopping to ease the pain in her arms and back. Once, she lay Andries down on the ground and stood up to stretch. She listened to see if she could hear the sound of the sea, which had been such a constant companion to them when they were at the camp, but there was no comforting sound of the pounding surf to tell her where it was. She stared in every direction but it all looked the same. Scrubby bushes, with the occasional grass tree and other stumpy trees to relieve the monotony. She tried to remember what François had said about how the natives made use of the grass tree, but her mind was confused. She knew she needed to drink more water but the water bottle was already low and she had hoped to save the best water for Andries and to find more pools in the rock surface, but there didn't seem to be any here.

Suddenly there was a sharp cry from the baby and she bent down to him.

There was a line of huge ants crawling over him and he was writhing and yelling in pain. Annie scooped him up in her arms again and tried to comfort him.

'I'm so sorry, Andries.' She brushed the ants away from him and one crawled up her arm and bit into her flesh. She almost dropped the baby in alarm.

'My poor baby,' she said. 'They have a vicious bite, do they not? No wonder you screamed.' She started to unwind the linen which held him fast and shook it out. Several more ants tumbled from its folds and now she felt them climbing up her legs, too.

'Oh God, I cannot be rid of them,' she muttered, walking away, striking at her legs and arms and shaking her skirt.

It wasn't such a big incident, but it was enough to break her resolve and she started to cry. The winter sun was strong and she was weak with thirst and with the difficult walking.

'I'm so sorry, Andries,' she whispered again. 'I thought it for the best. But now I am lost and we are alone; I don't even know how to retrace our steps to the camp. And I'm so frightened.'

The baby's cries had lessened but now he was whimpering pathetically in her arms. She rocked him from side to side, standing there in the bush, bewildered, not knowing in which direction to go. Her feet were sore in the ill-fitting shoes and her limbs were tired and heavy. She thought of François and Lucas and the others, heading away from her in the opposite direction. Were they faring better? Of course they were! They had plentiful supplies with them and François had learnt something of the natives' craft and, best of all, they had Melchior, who understood the winds and the stars. He would make sure they didn't get lost.

'I was a fool to leave so ill prepared,' she muttered to herself. Her mind was beginning to wander, from thirst, from lack of food and from exhaustion, but she stumbled on – and on. Sometimes she thought she heard voices but she soon came to realize that they were only in her head. She would hear her father laughing, teasing her – and May – and sometimes Susan, so recently dead, speaking calmly and sensibly to her as she had when Annie was a little girl. And Jacob's voice came through too, patiently explaining about the diseases he was treating, the importance of keeping a wound clean, and suchlike. But the clearest voice was François's. It came to her constantly and steadily, through the waves of nausea and faintness that were attacking her and through the pounding of her head.

I will never leave you, Annie.

But you have, François. You *have* left me.

The baby was silent now, limp in her arms, arms that were almost too weak to carry him. She was no longer aware of where she was walking and, once, she tripped over, instinctively shielding Andries from the impact of the ground but he hardly reacted, giving only the faintest mewl. She lay where she was for a while, knowing she should keep going and having to force herself to get to her feet again. At last she staggered upright, lurching forward, making little progress. She was either shivering with cold or flushed with heat. She felt dizzy and the scenery in front of her sometimes advanced and sometimes receded, and this frightened her more than the darkening sky.

'I can't get sick. I must keep going.' It was a mantra that she repeated to herself, again and again, though it was not said out loud, for her throat was too dry to form any words.

The sun was low now, but she was too muddled and confused to make sense of its direction. On and on she stumbled, falling more and more often, the silent, limp baby too weak to make any objection. And then, suddenly, it was dark and she could no longer see anything in front of her. But still she continued, forcing herself forward with frenzied determination, long after her body had told her to stop.

Until she fell again, and this time she could not get up; she lay whimpering on the ground, fighting the feeling of faintness as long as she could, the silent baby still strapped to her chest. But finally she was overwhelmed and they lay there, she and Andries, exposed and uncovered.

As the darkness deepened, Annie drifted in and out of consciousness, but she was never aware enough to crawl under the shelter of a bush. Several times during the night, she thrashed her arms from side to side and cried out in her delirium, but still the baby did not stir.

She was unaware, too, of the storm brewing up at sea which then swept inland, and of the rain that lashed them during the night.

When dawn broke, neither Annie nor Andries stirred.

It was not long after daybreak that a group of hunters from a local tribe came upon them. They walked round Annie, poking at her curiously with their spears and talking and gesticulating among themselves. Frequently they pointed up to the sky. Then one of them squatted down beside her and turned her over; it was only then that they saw the baby. Carefully, the man unstrapped the baby from Annie's chest and picked him up, frowning and touching his pallid skin, then he put his ear to the baby's chest and, sensing the faintest of flutters from Andries's heart, spoke excitedly to his companions.

The tribesmen conferred together for a while, then one of the others leaned down and picked up Annie's slight, limp, drenched body and gently slung her over his shoulder.

The men were barefoot but they moved gracefully over the rough ground, never breaking stride. As the sun rose higher in the sky, they stopped by a small rock pool which had filled from the rain of the night, and drank some water. Annie had drifted back to consciousness once or twice but she was too weak to take in where she was or what was happening to her. The man carrying her lowered her to the ground and put handfuls of water to her lips, grunting at her, urging her to drink. She opened her eyes and shrank away from him in fear of his broad dark face and unruly hair, so close to her face, and the sharp smell of his body reaching her nostrils, but she did manage to take a little water, though her dry and swollen lips made it difficult to swallow. Still delirious, she thrashed her head from side to side, knowing she must look for something but not remembering what it was. Then, another of the tribesmen held out Andries to her and she stretched out her arms, groaning, but then fell back, limp and useless.

The blacks talked and gesticulated among themselves and one tried to get some water into the baby's mouth but by now Andries's head was lolling and his whole body seemed lifeless. One of the men listened, again, to his chest and, frowning, moved away. But another came forward to listen and made further gestures. This man forced the baby's jaws apart and gently used his other hand to trickle water down his throat. To their surprise, there was some reaction. A faint splutter. Excitedly, they all gathered round then and, bit by bit, they poured more water into his mouth. A lot of it just soaked his linen wrap, but some made it down his throat and there was another choking sound as he automatically swallowed a little.

They forced more water down Annie's throat, too, holding her down when she struck out at them, not conscious of what she was doing. Then, pausing only to take water for themselves, they continued on their journey.

It was almost a day's walk from the place where Annie had collapsed and the sun was low in the sky when the group of men arrived at their camp. They were immediately surrounded by others, who stared at Annie as her carrier laid her gently on the ground.

There were some white men among the blacks – some of the seamen and soldiers who had deserted. They, too, stared at Annie.

'Has she come on her own?' said one.

Another shook his head. 'It is a foolhardy venture

for a young lass and a babe. Where's her mother? Has she died?'

And then, someone else pushed through the crowd. It was the young nursing mother who Annie had met earlier and who had been so delighted with Andries.

She didn't need telling. She understood immediately why Annie was there and why she had struck out on her own with the baby.

Wordlessly, she took the half dead child from the arms of his rescuer and put him to her breast.

Chapter Sixteen

Melchior, François and the others were making steady progress, even though the going was rough and on that stormy night, like Annie, they were lashed by the wind and rain. They had hardly used their water bottles but had drunk water from the soak the natives had shown François and then again, from rock pools that had filled with rainwater. They, too, had to make detours round gorges, but Melchior's sense of direction served them well and he assured them that they were heading south towards the great river which was their goal.

At one point they met up with a group of native hunters and this time the men did not run away from them. Melchior sat down and stretched out his arms towards them, as he had done before, and the natives joined him, gesticulating and chatting.

'Word must have spread among them,' whispered François to Lucas. 'They are no longer so fearful of us.'

Melchior found a patch of flat rock and drew a rough picture of a river on it. The men looked at it but didn't react. Melchior kept smiling at them and pointing forward. They didn't seem to understand, but when Melchior made to get up and move on again, the natives came with them. After a little while, Melchior told his men to drop back and follow the blacks. This was a wise move, because they led the group via tracks which the white men wouldn't have identified, making their going much faster – though all of them, strong as they were, found it hard to keep up with the loping, sure footed pace of their guides.

They accompanied Melchior and the others for about half a day and then the natives stopped abruptly at a large gorge. Melchior and the others thought they were stopping to rest, but it appeared that the natives wouldn't go any further. They lined up along the edge of the gorge, pointing the way forward, and then they turned back the way they'd come.

Melchior watched them go and then ordered his party to rest for a while and take some food. Lucas was glad that the party had halted. Being younger and smaller than the others, he had found the going tougher, but he never complained. He went and sat near François while one of the other men handed out a few supplies.

'Why did the blacks stop here?' he asked.

François shrugged. 'Who knows? Perhaps this marks the end of their territory.'

It was less than half a day's walking when they had their first sight of the river, but when finally they looked down upon it, everyone's spirits lifted. It was a magnificent, wide, fast flowing river surrounded by towering cliffs and gorges.

They all stopped, then, to admire it and Melchior shaded his eyes to look more carefully at the river's edge, to where they might build a camp. The sky was clear and blue again, and the colours – the reds and ochres of the cliffs and the shifting blue and green of the river – danced in the sunlight.

Lucas looked from right to left, in awe of the sight before them. Suddenly he saw something far away, upriver. At first he thought he had imagined it but then he looked again. He put his hand on François's arm. 'Look. There's smoke.'

They all looked then. 'Well spotted, Lucas,' said Melchior, smiling. 'You have sharp eyes.'

'Does that mean there is a native camp there, sir?' asked Lucas.

Melchior nodded. 'Aye, I would imagine so.' He

rubbed his bearded chin thoughtfully. 'Let us hope that they are friendly.'

It took them the rest of the day to reach the river's edge and they made camp as soon as they arrived. As they sat round the fire, Melchior addressed them.

'We have achieved our goal, men, but now comes the difficult part.'

Lucas smiled to himself. He'd never been addressed as a man before. Melchior went on. 'Tomorrow we shall explore the river bank and try to make contact with the natives. Pray God they will be friendly and show us where we should settle.' He turned to François. 'Do you think that is a wise plan, François?'

François was flattered to be consulted. 'Aye,' he said slowly. 'Aye, I think it would be wise to show ourselves to them and try to befriend them.' He shifted his weight from one side to the other, trying to get comfortable. 'We do not want to offend them. If *they* show us where to camp then it *will* be in a place which will not offend them.'

'Wise words from such a young head,' said Melchior. François blushed at the praise. Before he settled down to sleep he went to stand at the water's edge and listened to the sound of the river. They could make a good camp here. There was food and water to be had – and shelter, by the look of it. Yes indeed, it was a grand place to settle; and Pieter would build a boat and they would sail back to Java. All the survivors at the wreck site would come here and they would be together again.

His last thought, before he went to sleep that night, was of Annie, and he sent a silent prayer up for her: *Please, God, keep her safe.*

The next morning, François awoke to the sound of screeching birds in the trees behind him and he turned to see red and green flashes as the birds flew noisily about. He got up and stretched, filled with relief that they had reached this blessed river. Here they could live reasonably well; he was sure of that.

Melchior was already busy making plans.

'François, you and Pieter are to come with me and we will go upriver in search of the native camp.'

So, when they had had a little food and filled their water bottles from the river, the three of them set off, keeping to the river bank as much as they were able.

The native camp was further away than they thought but at last they came round a bend in the river and saw the curl of smoke rising up into the cloudless sky.

'We don't want to frighten them,' said Melchior. 'We mustn't steal up on them and surprise them.'

He needn't have worried. The natives had seen them coming and already they were flitting silently in among the trees, observing them as the white men advanced slowly on the camp. But the natives were so quiet, so stealthy, that Melchior and the others noticed nothing. As his party came nearer, they could see that it was quite a large native settlement and it had a permanent look about it. The huts were sturdy and well built and there seemed to be some sort of cultivation going on beside the encampment.

Melchior, Pieter and François stopped and stood still a little way away from the huts. At first, the natives just stared at them but then a few men broke through the crowd and walked towards them. They were armed with spears and shields. Instinctively, François bowed his head in greeting, even though his heart was hammering against his chest. Melchior stretched his hands out towards them in the submissive greeting he had used before – and to show that he was unarmed. Pieter stood behind the other two, his eyes darting nervously from side to side.

One of the men stepped forward and took hold of Melchior's tattered jacket. Melchior stood his ground and tried to remain calm. The native pulled at one of the buttons on the jacket and then thrust it back again. Melchior turned to François. 'Have you got the trinkets I gave you?' he whispered.

François nodded and stepped forward. Out of his pocket he produced a few loose buttons, a buckle and a book clasp and gave them to Melchior. Slowly, with much ceremony, Melchior handed them to the oldest of the three natives. As before, the man smelt the gifts and bit them but then seemed to lose interest in them. But after this exchange, he signalled the visitors to follow him to the centre of the camp and to sit down by the fire.

As Melchior did his best to explain through gestures and through drawing on the sandy ground where they had come from and what they needed, François and Pieter looked around them. Pieter took careful note of the construction of the huts with their walls of sticks woven through with bark and plastered with mud, the roofs made from clods of earth also plastered with mud to keep the weather out; François, meanwhile, was more interested in looking at the people. They were a little different from the natives they had encountered so far and François wondered if they were, indeed, of a different tribe, but what intrigued him most was that some of them were a lot less dark than others and had lighter hair and eyes.

At last, Melchior had made some sort of breakthrough and a few of the tribesmen came with them back to where they had made camp on the river bank. If the natives were afraid at the sight of white men, they didn't show it, but picked up some of the unfamiliar objects such as the tinderbox and stared at the men's shoes and the musket, which was propped up against a tree.

By evening, much progress had been made. The natives had indicated to them a good place to make camp and shown them how to trap fish with a net woven from vines, and then, as the sun started to sink towards the horizon, they suddenly left, without saying anything to each other or to the white men, and went back upriver.

Once they had left, Pieter stretched. 'Well,' he said, 'I can make huts as good as theirs – a deal better, even.' He looked round at the sandy depression surrounded by trees, the spot chosen for them by the natives. 'This is a good place to make camp,' he continued. 'And we have space to build a craft, too.'

Melchior smiled. 'And launch her,' he said, glancing through the trees at the river. 'It is a good place indeed.' He turned to François. 'What do you say, Mr Midshipman?'

François was still thinking about the natives they had seen and puzzling over them. 'Aye,' he said. 'It is.' Then he added, 'Did you notice the pale skinned folk among the natives?'

Melchior nodded. 'I did.'

'And were you wondering?'

'Wondering if they were the descendants of the two *Batavia* mutineers? Aye, I was.'

'They could have been, could they not?'

Melchior nodded. 'They were marooned in these parts some eighty years ago. It is possible they became part of the local tribe.'

'Then perhaps some of these natives know some Dutch words,' said François.

'Aye. Maybe. Doubtless we shall find out, by and by.'

The next few days were busy ones for the eight men. The trees near the river were more sturdy and Pieter had brought a salvaged axe with him so that they were able to cut down small branches and, having examined the natives' huts, they wove the long strips of bark which hung from some of the trees through the upright sticks to make walls and plastered them over with mud dug from the river.

Lucas worked tirelessly, eager to prove his usefulness to the others, and even Pieter, a man of few words, praised him.

'You are a handy lad, Lucas,' he said, patting him on the back, and Lucas blushed with pleasure.

There were plenty of fish in the river and there was plenty of fresh water too, and they even managed to trap some of the dragon-like creatures, shoot birds with bows and arrows fashioned by Pieter and the others, and shoot the hopping furry creatures with the musket.

'We must learn to kill the beasts without using the musket,' said Melchior. 'There is only a limited supply of shot. We must learn from the natives.'

Most days, the natives appeared to watch their progress. Sometimes they brought gifts of shells or grubs or another spear and the white men would try and find something to give them in return. François spent more time with them than the others, communicating in gestures and slowly beginning to recognize the common words. He would repeat them over and over, while the native men laughed at him and pointed and then, if he got the word right, would nod with pleasure and laugh again. Among the party there was one very light skinned young man and occasionally François would say Dutch words to him to see if there was any recognition. But the only time he got a reaction from him was when François had cut his thumb while whittling away at an arrow and swore. The young man's eyes lit up and he immediately repeated the swearword.

Soon, though, François became restless. He was anxious to get back to the cliff top camp and to fetch Annie and the others. Frequently he asked Melchior if he could take a party back, but Melchior was not to be hurried.

'Wait until we have huts for them, François,' he said. 'And we shall need to decide what to bring here from the campsite, too.'

'Aye,' interrupted Pieter. 'For a start we'll need as much driftwood as they can carry, and sailcloth, too, if we are to build a boat.'

So François had to be patient, but at last the day came when Melchior called the men together.

'It is time to go back and fetch the others,' he said. 'François, you are to come with me.'

François grinned broadly. 'Yes, sir,' he said.

'And young Lucas, too,' added Melchior.

Lucas looked astonished. 'Me, sir?' he said.

Melchior smiled. 'Aye, Lucas, you are the sharpest eyed among us. It will be useful to have you with us.'

So the next day the three of them set off again, fitter and more full of optimism than on their previous journey, and because there were only three of them and they had less to carry and were better at seeking out animal tracks, they made good progress despite the dense bush and were in sight of the cliff top campsite after two days.

François couldn't keep the stupid smile from his face as they approached. Annie would be there; they would be together again and he would take her to the great river from where they could escape back to Java.

Jan Liebent had seen them approach and he went out to greet them. He clapped Melchior on the back.

'I thought never to see you again, my friend,' he said,

ignoring the presence of François and Lucas. François smiled inwardly. Jan's animosity towards Melchior seemed to have melted away now that he was back. Perhaps he realized now how important Melchior was, not only with his knowledge of the sea and stars but also because the men all trusted him.

They had reached the site now and François looked around. Why had Annie not come to greet them? Surely she would have heard their arrival? Excusing himself, he went to the tent where she and her mother had slept but there was no sign of them. He asked a seaman who was sitting on the ground gutting some fish. 'Have you seen Mistress Annie?' he asked.

The man looked up. 'Mistress Annie?' he said stupidly. 'Why, she's gone.'

François stood very still, suddenly numb with fear. A fear much greater than the fear he'd felt of the bush or the natives or even of storms and the sea. A visceral, miserable, overwhelming fear.

'What do you mean?' he said slowly.

The man sniffed and wiped his nose on the back of his hand.

'Disappeared,' he said. 'She and the babe. They went off one morning and no one's seen them since.'

Suddenly, François felt fury at the man's indifference. He squatted down opposite the man and put his hands on his shoulders and shook him, forcing him to look into his eyes.

'How can she have disappeared? What of her mother? Why has no one searched for her?'

'Calm yourself, midshipman,' said the man, wriggling from François's grasp. He sniffed again. 'They left not long after you and the others. The mother died, see – and the next day, the girl and the baby went. No one saw them go.'

François ran back to Melchior and Jan, who were now standing by the fire, deep in conversation.

'Where's she gone?' he shouted at Jan. 'What's happened to her? Has no one looked for her?'

Jan turned to him with a blank expression. 'Don't interrupt, midshipman,' he said coldly. But Melchior put a hand on François's shoulder. 'What is it? What's happened?'

François could hardly get the words out. 'She's gone!' he stuttered. 'Annie and the baby disappeared not long after we went.' Melchior looked shocked but Jan simply shrugged his shoulders.

'Probably for the best,' he said. 'This is no place for a young girl and a –'

He didn't finish the sentence, for François had flown at him in pure rage. 'How dare you!' he yelled. 'You unfeeling fool! How could you say that? And why did you not send someone to look for her? Why –'

Melchior pulled him off Jan. 'Enough, François,' he

said harshly. 'You forget yourself.'

Jan turned furiously on François. 'That is a breach of discipline, midshipman,' he began.

'But an understandable one,' said Melchior, and his eyes were cold when he addressed Jan.

François turned away. 'I'm going to find her,' he shouted back at the two men. But Melchior followed him. He put his hand on his arm and, although François shook it off, he did not move away.

'Think, François. She left weeks ago. She has almost certainly perished. She and the baby could not have survived for long in these harsh conditions. And remember that storm we had? She would have been out in that. It is hard, lad, but a search would be fruitless now. You must see that.'

'She may have found the native camp,' said François, stubbornly.

Melchior shook his head. 'We need you here, François. You are my right hand man. And,' he added, 'if we manage to build a boat and make it to Java, you know that your future will be bright. One day, I am convinced, you will command your own ship. Think of that, François.'

François looked at his feet. 'It would be a hollow achievement without her,' he muttered.

Melchior's voice hardened. 'Jan will order you to stay, François,' he said. 'You know that. And if you disobey and go looking for Annie then you will lose everything. You will not find her alive and then, when you rejoin us and if we make it to Java, Jan will report you and it will go ill for you with the authorities. And,' he added sternly, 'you know that I would have to back him up.'

François looked at him then and his eyes filled with tears. Angrily he wiped them away with the back of his hand.

Just before all the survivors left to go back to the river, Lucas went to the cliff's edge and slithered down to the beach. Finding the heaviest boulders that he could carry, he painstakingly wrote out a message with them on the sand. Gone south, it read. François had seen Lucas go and had followed him. He looked down from the cliff top and smiled. How proud Annie would have been of her pupil. He waited until Lucas was up on top of the cliff again and pointed to the message.

'Well done, Lucas,' he said.

'It is for Mistress Annie,' said Lucas. 'In case she comes this way again.'

François had to turn away to hide his tears.

Chapter Seventeen

The weeks and months went by. The party of some forty survivors from the *Zuytdorp* were well established, now, on the banks of the great river, in their sturdy huts, with enough to eat and drink. François hardly smiled these days, but he made himself useful and he spent more and more time with the natives, learning from them and, very slowly, beginning to understand the rhythm of their life and their customs and skills.

Pieter and his helpers, meanwhile, had constructed a sturdy boat and already he and some of the seamen had tried it out on the fast flowing river. The seasons came and went and it was early summer when Jan and Melchior decided that the time had come to set sail for Java. The craft could only take twenty folk safely.

Melchior, the steersman, obviously had to go, and Jan as the Company man. Pieter the carpenter was needed too, in case the boat was damaged and needed repair; and seamen to sail and steer it.

Jan Liebent also wanted François to accompany them but Melchior, strangely, was against it.

'He's a leader, Jan, and his rapport with the natives is excellent. He will be needed here until we can reach Java and get the Company to send a rescue ship.'

When he heard their decision, for the first time in weeks, François allowed himself a grim smile. Melchior had left him behind as a kindness. He knew that François would go looking for Annie.

Those left behind all gathered on the river bank to watch the boat set sail. The seamen rowed it out to the deepest part of the river and then the rudely patched sail was hoisted.

'Godspeed,' they shouted from the bank – and watched until the craft disappeared round a bend in the river.

François waited a few days before putting his plan into action. The boat, after all, might founder further downriver and the party return to make repairs. He wanted to be sure it was long gone.

He found Lucas and took him to one side. They walked upriver for a little while then François stopped and sat on a flat rock at the river's edge. It was already hot even though it was still morning; the survivors had learnt to shade themselves from the fierce sun after several suffered from severe sunburn, their flesh swollen and tender and the skin peeling off in strips. The summer also brought clouds of flies that crawled on the lips and eyes and buzzed constantly around them. Immediately François and Lucas sat down they were attacked by another unwelcome swarm of the insects.

'Lucas,' said François, 'I need to tell you something.'

The boy was busy swatting uselessly at the flies. It had become, as it had to all of them, an almost unconscious and constant movement of the hand in front of the face. But he was all attention.

François continued. 'Lucas, I am going to go north again to search for Annie.' He hesitated. 'I may be gone a long time.'

Lucas immediately turned to him, his face alight, the flies forgotten.

'Take me with you, sir; please take me with you!'

François smiled at the boy's eagerness. 'I intend to search until I find her,' he said quietly. 'Either dead or alive.'

'I don't care how long it takes,' said Lucas. 'I want to find her, too. Please let me come with you.'

François sighed. 'I know what she meant to you,

Lucas.' He threw a stone into the river and watched the splash. Then he went on, 'If you really want to come with me, then I should be glad of your company.'

Lucas clapped his hands. 'When shall we leave?'

'Soon,' said François. 'Soon, I promise you. I have done my duty here; I obeyed orders and came back, even though it broke my heart to do so. No one can give me orders now.'

'And if we find her we can bring her back here before the rescue ship arrives from Java,' said Lucas.

'Aye. If it ever comes,' said François quietly.

They set off two days later. François told one of the other midshipmen of their plans and he nodded. 'God go with you, François, and come back safely to us.'

'Aye,' said François. 'Aye, I shall be back.'

The bush held much less fear for François now. He marvelled at its summer colour, contrasting so vividly to the dullness of the winter scrub, and his ear was finely tuned to the noises of bush creatures and the presence of the natives. He knew, now, how to cope with the searing heat and how to follow animal tracks. He and Lucas walked in the early morning and then again later in the day when the sun was low in the sky. When they came across groups of natives, François did his best to communicate with them and, once, he and Lucas were made welcome at a camp, though the camp was not permanent and just a place where the hunters were resting up.

When they reached the cliff top camp they stayed there for the night. It was a sad sight. The bush had already grown over the places where the tents had been. They went down to the beach and stood at the wreck site. Driftwood and other items were still being brought in by the tide; the ship, even though she was out of sight, was still spewing her guts. When they climbed up the cliff again and stood looking down, they could see Lucas's message, still clear on the sand. Gone south.

'Shall I change it?' asked Lucas.

François smiled. 'No, Lucas. That is the best message to leave.'

François was glad to leave the cliff top camp; it held too many memories for him, empty now and full of ghosts. They travelled on, keeping in sight of the sea as much as they could and looking always for signs of native habitation.

Sometimes they would come across native hunters but François's questions about the white girl and the baby were not understood. However, one day they came upon a group of hunters who gave them a glimmer of hope. One rocked his arms in front of him as if comforting a baby, and pointed further north.

It was a small enough signal but it buoyed up their spirits and they continued their journey with renewed vigour.

It was a few days after this encounter that Lucas's sharp eyes noticed something unusual. 'Look, sir,' he said, pointing to the ground. 'There are many more tracks now. Does this mean that there are more natives about?'

François inspected the ground. 'You are right, Lucas. I have been so busy looking in front of me that I've not bothered to look at the ground. Perhaps one of these will take us to a larger camp.'

As they walked on, the main track became clearer. 'It is leading us somewhere,' muttered François. He grasped Lucas's arm. 'Melchior was right, Lucas, you have the sharpest eyes of all of us.' They began to walk more quickly and even though the scrub was denser and taller than it had been in the winter, they made good progress. They paused only to drink water from the bottles slung at their sides. François sniffed the air. 'Can you smell smoke, Lucas?' he asked. 'Or is it my imagination?'

Lucas sniffed, too. 'You are right. There's a fire not far away.'

They exchanged glances and pressed on.

The smell of smoke became stronger but it was

quite a time later that they had their first glimpse of the large native encampment. There were many huts, though these were less well built than those at the riverside, and there was a mass of people, many squatting close to a huge waterhole, pounding seeds between grindstones or fetching water in large shells.

For a few moments, François and Lucas stood staring at the scene and then Lucas suddenly gasped. 'There are some white men here!' he said, pointing to a group of half naked men with pale skin.

François had seen them too and his heart started to beat very fast. 'Those men are some of the deserters,' he said. 'And maybe, if they are here, then . . .'

'Then Mistress Annie is here, too!'

Lucas started forward but François pulled him back. 'Take care, Lucas – we don't know how welcome we will be.'

But his warning was too late. They had been spotted and immediately there was a shouting and pointing and those squatting at the well straightened up to look.

François and Lucas walked forward. The first to meet them were the white men, looking ferocious and wild. They weren't pleased to see the visitors.

'Come to arrest us, have you, lad?' sneered one. 'Well, we're happy here and we ain't coming back.'

François found his voice. 'No,' he said quietly. 'No, we've come on another mission.'

'Oh yeah? What's that, then?'

But suddenly François couldn't speak. He had seen a group of children playing not far away, and among them was a white toddler.

God be praised, she must be here, he thought, and he started to run forward, oblivious to the crewmen's questions. It was left to Lucas to answer them.

'We've come to seek Mistress Annie,' said Lucas, watching as François reached the group of children.

There was silence from the men and Lucas looked from one to the other. 'Why? What's happened to her? Is she not here?' He pointed to the group of children. 'Surely that's her brother?'

'Aye,' said one of the sailors quietly. 'That's her brother.'

Lucas frowned. 'Then where . . . ?'

'She didn't survive, lad,' said the man, putting a rough hand on Lucas's shoulder. 'She was brought here unconscious by the hunters and she died of the fever a few days later.'

Lucas stared at the man, unable to speak. How could fate strike such a cruel blow? Had they come so far only to find that Annie had died?

'But the baby lives,' he stuttered at last. It was a statement, not a question.

'Aye. The baby was half dead, too, but a native girl nursed him back to health.' The man turned to look at

Andries, crawling among his black playmates. 'He's a fine lad.'

Lucas stumbled over to François, who was squatting on the ground beside Andries. François leaned forward to pick up the baby but as he did so, a young woman rushed over and scooped Andries into her arms, holding him tightly and glaring at François. François looked up, startled, and as he did so, he saw a leather pouch tied around the young woman's neck. He let out a cry and stretched out his hand to touch it but the girl jumped back. It was Annie's pouch, the one given her by Jacob; it was her most precious possession. For a moment François felt pure elation, but then he frowned. Why? Why was this native girl wearing Annie's pouch?

Lucas was at his side now and François turned to him. 'Look, Lucas,' he said excitedly, pointing to the pouch. 'It's Annie's!'

Lucas swallowed. Tentatively, he put out his hand to touch François – and then withdrew it.

'She's gone, sir,' he said quietly.

'Gone? Who has gone? What do you mean?'

'Mistress Annie. The sailors told me.' Lucas could feel his eyes welling up. 'She died of the fever,' he said.

François got slowly to his feet and Lucas could hardly bear to see the pain in his face. He'd expected François to rage at the unfairness of it, to shout out and curse, but he simply stood there staring at Lucas, unwilling to believe it but knowing it to be true. Annie wasn't here. If she'd been here he would have sensed her presence as soon as he entered the camp; and if she'd been here she would have sensed his and run to him.

Miserably, he watched the native girl; she was a little way away from them now, playing with Andries.

Lucas followed his gaze. 'That young woman,' he said quietly. 'She's saved the baby's life.'

François didn't answer for a while. The young woman had, indeed, saved Andries's life, but Annie had, too, by bringing him here. And by doing that . . .

'And yet they couldn't save Annie,' he said, his voice breaking. 'She gave her life for her brother's.'

He turned away from Lucas and put his head in his hands.

Later, one of the sailors led them to the natives' burial site, an hour's walk south-east of the camp.

'They buried her over there,' he said gruffly, pointing to a sandy ridge covered in vegetation flattened by the strong southerly winds.

François asked to be left alone and when Lucas and the sailor were out of sight, he knelt down in the sand facing the ridge, and spoke softly into the wind.

'What dreams we had, Annie,' he said.

He stayed there a long time and once he fancied

that he heard her voice again, borne on the sea breeze. 'I love you, François.'

'And I you, Annie,' he replied. 'But you never knew how much.'

Later, as the sun was beginning to sink beneath the dunes, he stood up, his limbs stiff.

'I promised once that I would never leave you, Annie,' he said, 'and I broke that promise, but I swear to God that this time I shall honour it. I shall never leave you again.'

When Lucas saw that François had risen to his feet, he ran to him. Lucas was crying openly and François put an arm around the boy's shoulders.

'Will you stay here with us, Lucas?' he asked, his voice husky. 'Will you stay here with Annie and me?'

Lucas looked up through his tears. 'And with Andries?'

'Aye. And with Andries.'

Afterword

Although it is known that there were survivors from the *Zuytdorp*, no one knows exactly what happened to them. They certainly made camps on the beach (local tribes passed this information down through the generations) and on the cliff top, where many artifacts were found – and it is very likely that they integrated with local tribes; a tobacco box lid was found at what was once a large Aboriginal settlement at Wale Well, north of the wreck site. It is also possible that the survivors settled beside the Murchison River and built a boat in which they set sail for Java. However, if they did make their escape by boat they must have perished at sea, for the *Zuytdorp*'s crew and passengers were never heard of again. The wreck of the ship was first discovered in 1927 but it was only positively identified as the *Zuytdorp* in the 1950s, by the date of the silver coins still at the site.

The 'ancient city' in the story is the famous Pinnacles near the modern town of Cervantes. These are thousands of huge, ancient rock pillars made up of shells and rising from the desert, from the time when the sand there was beneath the sea. They can, indeed, be seen from the sea, and ancient mariners could be forgiven for thinking that they were the ruins of an ancient city.

Historical Background

The *Zuytdorp* was one of the largest VOC ships. She had already made two successful trips to the East Indies and Asia when she left Holland in July 1711. She was accompanied by the *Belvliet*, a much smaller ship, also on her third voyage. On board the *Zuytdorp* were 286 people – a hundred soldiers, four tradesmen and 182 others, mainly seamen, but including several cabin passengers. The cabin passengers included some women and children.

Marinus Wysvliet was the skipper of the *Zuytdorp*. He had not commanded a VOC ship before, whereas Dirck Blaauw, skipper of the *Belvliet*, had previously commanded two vessels on voyages to Asia. It seems unusual that Blaauw was not appointed skipper of the *Zuytdorp*, the larger and more valuable ship. However, because of his seniority, he was appointed 'skipper in command' of the two ships on their voyage to the Cape of Good Hope.

As well as wine, beer, butter, meat, bacon, lead ingots, cloth, rope, sulphur, pitch, canvas, paper, muskets, leather, copper, salt, iron hoops and plates, the *Zuytdorp* was also carrying a huge amount of newly minted coins to use in purchasing trade goods in Asia.

Initially, the weather was dreadful; rough seas and a lot of fog. The two ships were part of a fleet of thirteen which included two vessels going out loaded with food and drink to meet an incoming fleet returning to Holland from the East. When news came that this fleet had already arrived back in Holland, Wysvliet and Blaauw requested that some of the additional food and drink from the supply ships be transferred to the *Zuytdorp* and the *Belvliet*. This was done, and charged to the Company's account.

There is something odd about this. They had only been at sea for three weeks, having left with supplies to last six months, and it has been suggested that the two skippers might have hoped to profit from the illicit sale of the surplus food after the ships reached Java. This was apparently not unusual.

There were also well founded rumours that 'Wysvliet ill treated his people and gave them all but nothing to eat.' This may well have been a factor in the ill health on board (see below).

The ships made reasonably good progress until they reached the belt of very light winds and still weather along the equator known as the doldrums, where they were effectively becalmed. By this time the death toll on board both ships was unusually high and many other crew members were very sick, so the decision was taken to sail east towards the African coast and put in at the island of São Tomé in the Gulf of Guinea, in search of fresh food and water. The crew also cut wood while on land.

Because of the windless conditions, it took weeks to reach São Tomé and, altogether, this diversion delayed the journey by about three months. After leaving São Tomé, the ships became separated and during the trip down to the Cape, the skipper of the *Belvliet*, Dirck Blaauw, died and the master surgeon of the *Zuytdorp* committed suicide. The ships finally reached the Cape of Good Hope in March 1712 within a few days of one another, having taken eight months to get there – double the normal time.

There were 166 people still alive on the *Zuytdorp* when she reached the Cape. Eight were cabin passengers ('cabin guests') and 158 crew. Of these, twenty-two were listed as sick.

Having recruited replacement crew at the Cape and

taken on fresh supplies (only when persuaded to – the skipper boasted that he needed very little to make the journey on to Java, thus, presumably, saving himself some money!) the *Zuytdorp* left, this time in company with a different ship (the *Kockenge*) on 22 April 1712, to sail to Java. These two ships were supposed to keep together but the *Zuytdorp* soon pulled ahead and disappeared from sight, never to be seen again.

Had the skippers of the *Zuytdorp* and the *Belvliet* survived, it is certain that they would have been taken to task when they reached Java for the diversion they made into the Gulf of Guinea. About two thirds of all fatalities during the voyage to the Cape of Good Hope happened in the three months spent in the Gulf of Guinea.

The Shipwreck

For centuries, nothing was known of the fate of the *Zuytdorp*, but in 1958 it was established beyond doubt that it came to grief in the (Australian) winter of 1712, between the mouth of the Murchison River and Shark Bay, at the foot of the coastal cliffs that now bear its name.

The Survivors

That there were survivors is undisputed though,

of course, no one knows how long they survived or whether they integrated with the local Aboriginals. The VOC archives in The Hague in Holland estimate that around seventy people survived the wreck. Other sources put the figure either much lower or much higher. On a beach south of the wreck site, there was evidence of a fire and on top of the cliffs there was also evidence of campsites. Artifacts found at these cliff top campsites included glass, pipes, barrel rungs and coins – and there were also *Zuytdorp* relics found at Aboriginal wells in the region north and inland from the wreck site. A Dutch tobacco box lid and buttons were found at Wale Well, where a large group of Aboriginal people lived long before white settlement.

In 1834, not long after white settlement, Aboriginal men from 'Waylo' (the Wale Well area) told stories of white men coming from the sea who gave food in exchange for spears and shields. They also described 'houses' – two large and three small – situated on the open coast and made of wood and canvas and of 'tall white men with women and children'. But the most distinctive feature of the wreck site, repeated many times by the informants, was of a great deal of 'white money' (silver coins) scattered along the shore in front of the wreck. These stories had been passed down from generation to generation and from tribe to tribe. The sudden appearance of this shipwreck and of the white people who scrambled ashore, must have had a huge impact on the Aboriginal people of the area. A story of this major event would certainly have been handed on during the 122 years from 1712 to 1834.

The Aboriginals in the area would also have known about the two mutineers from the *Batavia* (Looes and Pelgrom) who were marooned not far away – near the mouth of the Murchison River – some eighty years earlier, and their reaction to the *Zuytdorp* survivors (friendly or otherwise) may have been influenced by the behaviour of these two white men. (See my book *The Blue-Eyed Aborigine*.)

Finally, early explorers to the area, shortly after European settlement, reported sightings of fair haired Aboriginals with 'distinctly Dutch features'.

It is very likely that some Dutch seamen and soldiers – and even passengers – from the *Zuytdorp* survived and integrated with the local tribes, and there is ongoing DNA research to establish a pre-settlement genetic link between the coastal tribes and Western Europeans.

List of Main Characters

On board the Zuytdorp:

Marinus Wysvliet*, skipper of the *Zuytdorp*.

Melchior Haijensz*, uppersteersman.

Jan Liebent, undermerchant.

Annie, Susan and Andries Jansz.

> Annie is the fifteen-year-old daughter of Susan and Andries Jansz, travelling as a 'cabin guest' to Java with her parents. Her father, Andries, is employed by the VOC and is to take up a post overseeing the Company's warehouses in Java.

May Pilman, woman servant to the Jansz family.

François Carel de Bruijn*, eighteen-year-old Norwegian midshipman.

> Well educated, from a wealthy family. On his first voyage – expected to follow an illustrious career with the VOC.

Lucas Decker, twelve-year-old ship's boy. Illiterate orphan.

Jacob Hendricx, master surgeon.

Other minor characters on board the *Zuytdorp* include a carpenter (Pieter Morreij uit Domburg*), a cook (Jan van de Kerkhoven*) and sundry sailors and soldiers (including Michel Swarts* and Baernt Dannekeand*). And the ship's cat!

On board the Belvliet:

> Dirck Blaauw*, skipper of the *Belvliet*.

Starred names are those of real people who were on board. All other names are fictional but they are names which would have been reasonably common in the seventeenth and eighteenth centuries. There were more German than Dutch soldiers on board. Foreigners often joined Dutch ships as conditions on board were usually better than those of their native country.

NB: Zeeland was a province of the Dutch Republic.

About the Author

ROSEMARY HAYES lives and works in rural Cambridgeshire. She has written over forty books for children including historical and contemporary fiction and fantasy. Rosemary lived in Australia for six years and her first novel, Race Against Time, set in Australia, was runner-up for the Kathleen Fidler Award and since then many of her books have won, or been shortlisted for, other awards.

Her other books for Troika include *The Blue-Eyed Aborigine*, also set in Australia, and *The Mark*.

To find out more about Rosemary:
Visit her website www.rosemaryhayes.co.uk
Follow her on twitter @HayesRosemary
Read her blog at www.rosemaryhayes.co.uk/wpf

'A gripping adventure story that raises timeless questions about human behaviour, conditioning and ultimately the power of love.'
Magpies

'A superbly written story centring around the 17th century Dutch atrocity that occurred off the coast of Western Australia.'
Amazon

Shortlisted for The Young Quill Award, The West Australian Young Readers' Award and The Amazing Book Award.

'Hayes gets the tone, pace and action just right. Jan's story is gripping. Straight on to the school readings lists for this one, and for the best possible reasons.'
The Australian

The Blue-Eyed Aborigine

Rosemary Hayes

There is mutiny in the air . . .

In 1629 the Dutch ship *Batavia* plies her way towards
Java with her precious cargo. Cabin boy Jan and
Wouter, a young soldier, find themselves caught up
in a tragic shipwreck and a desperate struggle for
survival on the Houtman Abrolhos islands.

In this fast-moving story based on real events
Rosemary Hayes imagines the unknown – the lives,
relationships and discoveries of the two marooned
young Dutchmen as as they attempt to settle in a
country so different from their native Holland.

Two teenagers on the run from the past.

ROSEMARY HAYES

'The tension never flags and the ending is as surprising as it is brilliant' *The Irish Examiner*

'Totally and utterly gripping' *Carousel*

'A brilliant book' *Teen Titles*

'A nail-biting novel for teen and YA. Hayes' characterisation, her skill at telling a story, the economy of her style and its crystal-clear clarity are very much on display here' Richard Brown

The Mark

Rosemary Hayes

She's his mark.
How had it happened? Gradually he'd got used to
her, been surprised by her. At first he'd resented her,
yet bit by bit she had insinuated herself into his life; she
was growing on him and he'd begun to think of them
as a couple, well, not that sort of couple, but these two
rudderless souls up against the world.

Rachel is in a bad way when Jack marks her out.
Homeless, alone, desperate for love – she's easy prey for
Adam, the man who claims to be her boyfriend. Jack
intervenes and soon they are on the run together, an
odd couple both haunted by voices in their heads, both
trying to escape the nightmares of their past lives.
The woods and fields along their road to London
provide an unexpected refuge, and Jack starts to
believe he can get Rachel to safety, but can he do it
before his time runs out?

'This prolific and diverse author . . . a real page
turner' Jane Wilson-Howarth

Discover more stories

you'll love

at

troikabooks.com

 **#troikabooks**

troika